"It Won't Work."

"What won't?" Thalia asked. She had the nerve to look innocent.

"Trying to convince me to take the part. It won't work."

He had her full attention—and that was becoming a problem. Her eyes were wide-open, her lips were barely parted. All he'd have to do was lower his head.

Against his every wish, his head began to dip.

He could *not* kiss her; he could *not* be turned on by her; he could *not* be interested in her—but he was. She was going to ruin the life he'd made, and he almost didn't care. It was almost worth the way she looked at him, soft and innocent and waiting to be kissed.

Almost.

Dear Reader,

Welcome to the Bar-B Ranch, home of one of the hottest
heroes I've written, J.R. Bradley. J.R. has a secret, you
see—he used to be James Robert Bradley, the hottest actor
to come out of Hollywood since Brad Pitt. But he gave
up the fame and money—along with the constant scrutiny
and pressure—when he bought his own ranch and a whole
bunch of cows.

Since then, J.R. has been—well, he wouldn't call it
hiding, but you get the idea. He's got peace, quiet, cows
and a surrogate family he trusts with his life. Yup, he's got
everything he ever wanted. Or so he thinks.

Into this carefully constructed life rolls Thalia Thorne, a
producer looking for James Robert Bradley to star in a
new Western movie. J.R. says *no* in no uncertain terms—
but then a blizzard forces both of them to reconsider
their positions. While the temperatures plummet outside,
things inside get very hot. Suddenly J.R. finds himself
questioning his entire existence. When the ground thaws,
will he let Thalia leave? Or will he go with her?

A Real Cowboy is a hot story of accepting the past
and redefining the future. I hope you enjoy reading it
as much as I enjoyed writing it! Be sure to stop by
www.sarahmanderson.com and join me when I say
long live cowboys!

Sarah

SARAH M. ANDERSON

A REAL COWBOY

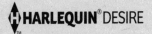

Recycling programs
for this product may
not exist in your area.

ISBN-13: 978-0-373-73224-1

A REAL COWBOY

Copyright © 2013 by Sarah M. Anderson

Printed in U.S.A.

Books by Sarah M. Anderson

Harlequin Desire

A Man of His Word #2130
A Man of Privilege #2171
A Man of Distinction #2184
A Real Cowboy #2211

SARAH M. ANDERSON

Award-winning author Sarah M. Anderson may live east of the Mississippi River, but her heart lies out West on the Great Plains. With a lifelong love of horses and two history teachers for parents, she had plenty of encouragement to learn everything she could about the Wild West.

When she started writing, it wasn't long before her characters found themselves out West. She loves to put people from two different worlds into new situations and see how their backgrounds and cultures take them someplace they never thought they'd go.

When not helping out at her son's elementary school or walking her rescue dogs, Sarah spends her days having conversations with imaginary cowboys and American Indians, all of which is surprisingly well tolerated by her wonderful husband. Readers can find out more about Sarah's love of cowboys and Indians at www.sarahmanderson.com.

To Robert and Nancy, the best in-laws
a woman could ask for. You don't often get to choose
your family, but even if I hadn't married their son,
I would have chosen them anyway.

One

The wheels of Thalia's rental sedan spun on the gravel as the driving winds tried to push her off the road, but she kept control of the car. It was nice to have control over something, even if it was a Camry.

Because she certainly did not have control over this situation. If she did, she wouldn't be stalking James Robert Bradley to the middle-of-nowhere Montana in what could only be described as the dead of winter. Hell, she didn't even know if she'd find him. And, as it had been close to an hour since she'd seen another sign of life, she wasn't sure she'd find anything.

Still, there was a road, and she was on it. Roads went places, after all. This one cut through miles and miles of Montana grassland that was probably lush and green in the summer. However, as it was late January, the whole landscape looked lifeless and deserted. Snow so old it had taken on a gray hue lined the road. If she were filming a postapocalyptic movie, this would be perfect.

At least it wasn't snowing right now, she told herself in a forcibly cheerful tone as she glanced at the car's thermometer. It was twenty-two degrees outside. Not that cold, really. She had that going for her. Of course, that didn't include the wind chill, but still. It wasn't like it was subzero out there. She could handle it.

Finally, she passed under a signpost that proclaimed Bar B Ranch, which also announced trespassers would be shot. The Camry's wheels bounced over a metal grate a part of her brain remembered was called a cattle guard. She checked the address she'd entered into her phone's GPS, and a sense of relief bum-rushed her. She was actually in the right place.

This realization buoyed her spirits. James Robert Bradley's agent, a small, nervous man named Bernie Lipchitz, hadn't wanted to give up the address on his most famous—and most private—Oscar-winning client. Thalia had been forced to promise Bernie she'd give his latest would-be starlet a role in the new movie she was producing, *Blood for Roses*.

Of course, it was her movie only as long as she could get James Robert Bradley signed for the part of Sean. If she couldn't do that…

No time to dwell on the worst-case scenario. She was making excellent progress. She'd tracked down Bradley's whereabouts, which was no easy task. She'd gotten onto his property—so far, without anyone shooting at her. Few people could claim to have gotten this close to Bradley since he'd disappeared from Hollywood after winning his Oscar almost eleven years ago. Now she had to sign him to the comeback role of a lifetime. Easy, right?

The clock on the dash said four o'clock, but the sun was already setting, shooting brilliant oranges and purples across the icy-blue sky. *Beautiful,* Thalia thought as the colors lit up the gray landscape. Off to what she thought was the north were a series of low hills that merged with taller mountains in the west. The south and east were as flat as a pancake.

She could almost see it in the full bloom of spring. The land was beautiful.

Maybe we could do some of the filming here, she thought as she rounded a bend and saw a massive structure that would have been called a log cabin, except *cabin* didn't do it justice. She couldn't tell if the huge, rough-hewn logs rose up two stories or three, and she also couldn't tell how far back the building went. Behind it were a number of barns—some with an old, weathered look, others made of gleaming metal. Except for the shiny metal buildings, everything looked like it had been on this patch of land for decades. If not centuries.

She didn't see a single living thing. Not even a dog ran up to greet her as she pulled in front of the house. A wide covered porch offered some protection from the wind.

Well, she wasn't going to get anyone signed to anything by sitting in a car. Gathering up all of her positive energy, she opened the door.

The icy wind nearly slammed the door shut on her leg and cut right through her patterned tights. *Dang,* she thought as she pushed against the door. Sure, it had been cold when she'd left the small airport terminal in Billings, Montana, to get into the car—but it hadn't been this cold. Suddenly, the knee-high boots and tights under the wool dress didn't seem like a smart business outfit making a concession to winter. They seemed like the definition of foolishness.

Bracing herself against the wind, she pulled the fur-lined collar of her wool trench coat up around her neck and trudged up the porch steps. *Please be home,* she thought as she looked for the doorbell. Her coat was not rated for this kind of weather.

Another blast of winter rushed up the back of her skirt, making her teeth chatter. Where was the doorbell? *Screw it,* she thought, pounding on the door in a most unprofessional way. Manners didn't matter when she was freezing to death.

No one answered.

Freezing to death—in Montana, of all places—wasn't on her to-do list today. Thalia couldn't remember being this cold, not even when she was a kid and spent all day playing in the rare snowstorm in Oklahoma. She'd lived in L.A. for the last ten years, for crying out loud. People there complained of the cold when it got below sixty.

Thalia banged on the door again, this time with both hands. Maybe someone was in there, she reasoned. The house was huge. Maybe they were in a room way in the back. "Hello?" She shouted, but the wind wasn't done with her yet.

No one came.

Okay, time to regroup. What were her choices? She could stand here on the porch until someone showed up, at the risk of freezing. She could try one of the barns. Maybe someone was feeding the animals, and if not, well, at least she'd be sheltered from the wind. The thin stiletto heels on her expensive boots made that a risky proposition. Still, better boots than her body. Or she could get back in the car, crank the heat and wonder what she'd done to deserve this.

Her foot was on the first step down when she saw them— two cowboys on horseback cresting one of the low hills. Thalia gasped at the image before her—it was perfect. The sunset backlit the riders, giving them a halo of gold. Clouds of fog billowed from each of the horse's noses, which made them look otherworldly. Powerful, with a hint of danger. The whole thing looked like something right out of a movie— and she would know. This is exactly how she wanted to introduce the character of Sean Bridger in *Blood for Roses*. She'd been right to push for signing James Robert Bradley. This was perfect. He was going to be *perfect*. She could see the Oscar nominations rolling in.

Plus, someone was here. She could go inside and warm up.

The riders slowed as one of them pointed in her general direction. She'd been spotted. Thank heavens. Much longer, and she wouldn't be able to feel her legs anymore. She gave a hopeful wave, one that said, "Hi. I'm cold." It must have worked, because one rider broke off and came charging toward the house at full speed.

Her optimism flipped over to fear in a heartbeat. This guy didn't look like he was coming to greet her—he rode like he was going to run her down. Sure, Bradley didn't want to be found—but he or whoever that was wouldn't *hurt* her, would he? This wasn't about to become a shoot-first-ask-later situation, was it? As quickly as she could without betraying her terror, she stepped back onto the porch and out of the line of those hooves.

Still, the rider came on at full speed, pulling up only when he was parallel with her rental. The horse, a shining palomino, reared back, hooves flailing as the steam from his mouth almost enveloped the two of them. The rider's long coat fanned out behind him, giving her a glimpse of fringed chaps. If she hadn't been so afraid, Thalia would have appreciated the artistry and sheer skill of the moment. As it was, she half expected to find herself looking down the barrel of a gun.

When the horse had settled down, the rider pulled the bandanna down. "Help you?" he said in the kind of voice that was anything but helpful.

Then she saw his eyes—the liquid amber that had been one of the defining characteristics of James Robert Bradley. She'd found him. The part of her brain that was still nineteen and watching him on the big screen in the movie *Hell for Leather* swooned, and swooned hard. God, she'd had the biggest crush on this man a decade ago. And now she was here, actually talking to *People* magazine's Sexiest Man Alive. Sure, that had been thirteen years ago, but those eyes were still just as dreamy. She fought the urge to ask him for his autograph. The man was intimidating the hell out of her.

Not that she'd let him know that. The first rule of negotiating with actors was not to show weakness. Never let the other party know they held all the cards. So she sucked up what frozen courage she could and said, "James Robert Bradley?"

A look of weariness flashed over those beautiful eyes, then he said, "Miss, I'm not interested."

"That's only because you haven't heard—"

He cut her off with a wave of his hand. "I appreciate the offer, but you can be on your way now." He turned his mount toward one of the larger, newer barns.

"You didn't even listen to what I have to say!" She took off after him, her thin heels wobbling on the uneven terrain. "Your agent told me you'd—"

"I'm going to fire him for this," was the last thing she heard before Bradley disappeared into the barn.

Thalia pulled up. The wind was stronger in the middle of the drive, but she didn't think following Bradley into the barn was in her best interests. He hadn't even listened to the offer. How was she supposed to sign him to the movie when she couldn't even get a civil reply out of him? And if she couldn't sign him, how was she supposed to go into the office and tell her boss without losing her job?

She heard hoofbeats behind her, and turned to see the other rider approaching at a slow walk. "Howdy," the cowboy said, tipping his hat. "Said no, didn't he?"

Maybe it was the cold, or the blown plan, or the prospect of being unemployed in less than twenty-four hours. Whatever it was, Thalia felt her throat close up. *Don't cry,* she thought, because nothing was less professional than crying over a rejection. Plus, the tears would freeze to her face. "He didn't even listen to the offer."

The cowboy gave her a once-over. "I'd be happy to take the part, miss, providing there's a casting couch involved." Then he winked.

Was he…laughing at her? She shook her head. Maybe he was joking. She couldn't tell. "Thanks, but I was looking for—"

"An Oscar winner, yeah, I know. Wish I could help you, but…he's pretty set in his ways."

"Hoss," came a shout from inside the barn.

"Boss man's calling." The cowboy named Hoss seemed to feel sorry for her.

"Could I at least leave my card? In case he changes his mind?"

"You could try, but…"

"Hoss!" The shout was more insistent this time. Hoss tipped his hat again and headed toward the barn.

So much for making progress. Yes, she'd found Bradley, and yes, seeing those eyes of his was probably worth the trip. Everything else? The wind was blowing away her body heat, her career and her crush. If she got in that car and drove away, she'd have nothing left. Levinson would fire her butt for failing to deliver the goods, and she'd be blacklisted. Like last time, when her affair with Levinson had blown up in her face. She couldn't face having every professional door shut in her face a second time.

She needed Bradley in a way that had nothing to do with his eyes and everything to do with gainful employment.

At least the anger she currently felt was warm in nature. She'd lost contact with her toes, but she could still feel her fingers.

The barn door through which both men had disappeared slid shut.

This was her own fault, she realized. She was the one who had suggested Bradley for the role of Sean. She was the one who had convinced Levinson that even a recluse like Bradley wouldn't be able to turn down the comeback role of a lifetime. She was the one who had staked her career on something that seemed so simple—getting a man to say yes.

She was the one who had bet wrong. And now she had to pay the price.

She marched back up to the front door, her head held high.

That was the second rule of negotiations—never let them know they've won. Her hands were shaking, but she managed to get a business card out of her coat pocket and wedge it in the screen door. The whole time, she mentally tried to come up with some contingency plans. Maybe she'd caught Bradley at a bad time; she knew where he lived now, and she had his number. She could try again and again—as long as it took until he at least heard her out.

Thalia remained convinced that, if he would just listen to her pitch, he'd be interested in the role. Actors, as a rule, craved public adoration, and what could be better than an Oscar-worthy movie?

No, this wasn't over. Not by a long shot. Still, hypothermia was becoming a risk. She wished she could go inside and warm up her hands and feet before she tried to drive, but it didn't look like an invitation would be forthcoming. As she turned back to the Camry, she saw the headlights of another vehicle coming down the road. Someone else meant another opportunity to plead her case, so she put on her friendliest smile and waited.

A mud-splattered SUV rolled up, window down. Before the vehicle had even come to a stop, a woman with graying hair stuck her head out. "What are you doing outside?" she demanded.

"I was hoping to talk to Mr. Bradley." Thalia kept her voice positive.

The woman gazed out at the barn. When her attention snapped back to Thalia, she looked mad enough to skin a cat. "And he left you out here? That man…" She shook her head in disgust. "Poor dear, you must be frozen. Can you wait long enough for me to pull around back and get the door open, or do you need to get in the car?"

Thalia loved this woman more than any other person in the whole world right now, because she was going to let Thalia inside. But she didn't want this stranger to know how cold she was—or how long she'd been stuck in this frozen purgatory. "I can wait." Her teeth chattered.

Without another word, the woman drove off. Thalia tried stamping her feet to keep the blood going, but it didn't do much except send pain shooting up her legs. *Just a few more seconds,* she told herself.

However, it felt like several minutes passed with no movement from either inside the house or from the barn. *Should have gotten in the car,* she thought. Then the front door swung open, and the older woman pulled her inside.

"You're frozen stiff!" she said in a clucking voice as she wrapped Thalia in what felt like a bearskin and pulled her deeper into the house. Thalia didn't have time to take in her surroundings before she found herself plunked down in a plush leather chair. Before her was a fire burning brightly in a massive stone fireplace that took up most of a wall.

Rubbing her hands together, she scooted forward to soak up the heat.

"I'm Minnie Red Horse, by the way. Let's get those boots off you. Nice boots, but not the best for winter out here."

"Thalia. Thorne." That was all she could get out as her blood began to pump through her frozen extremities. When Minnie pulled the boots off, Thalia couldn't keep the cry of pain out of her voice.

"Poor dear. You sit there and warm up. I'll make you some tea." Minnie stood and pulled the mesh covers off the fireplace before she stoked the logs. The flames jumped up, and Thalia felt closer to human.

"Thank you. So much." She managed to look at what she was wearing. Definitely an animal skin, which kind of creeped her out, but it was warm, so she ignored whatever PETA would say about it.

She heard Minnie shuffling around behind her. Thalia managed to sit up enough to look around. She was at one end of a long room. Behind her was a plank table, big enough to seat six. Beyond that was an open kitchen with rustic cabinets and a lot of marble. The whole effect was like something out of *Architectural Digest*—and far beyond the small ranch house her grandpa had spent his whole life in.

As big as the place seemed, it had looked much larger from the outside. Minnie had a kettle on. "Where are you from, Thalia?"

"Los Angeles." She tried wiggling her toes, but it still hurt, so she quit.

"You're a long way from home, sweetie. How long you been traveling?"

Thalia decided she liked Minnie, above and beyond the warm fire and the tea. It'd been a long time since anyone had called her *sweetie*. Not since Grandpa had died. Mom was more fond of *dear*. "My flight left LAX at 3:30 this morning."

"Goodness, you made that whole trip in one day?" Minnie walked over and handed Thalia a steaming mug. "That's quite a journey. Where are you staying tonight?"

"Um…" She'd had a plan, but her head was fuzzy right now. "I have a room in Billings."

Minnie gave her a look that landed somewhere between concern and pity. "You realize that's five hours away, and it's already near sunset, right? That's a long drive in the dark."

Thalia hadn't realized how far away Billings was from the Bar B Ranch when she'd booked the room, and given her current state, five hours seemed like five days. How was she going to make it that far? The drive out had been hard enough, and that had been during daylight hours. Fighting that wind in the dark on strange roads was kind of a scary thought.

"Here's what you're going to do." Minnie patted her arm after Thalia took several sips of the tea. "You're going to sit right here until you feel better, and then you're going to have dinner. You came through Beaverhead, right?"

Thalia nodded, trying not to snicker at the juvenile name. Minnie's tone made it clear that dinner was nonnegotiable, but Thalia wasn't sure she could have hopped up and bailed if she'd tried. Her toes *hurt*.

"Lloyd has rooms he rents—as close as we've got to a motel 'round these parts." Thalia didn't have a clue as to what Minnie was talking about, but she was in no position to argue. She took another sip of tea, loving the way the warmth raced down her throat and spread through her stomach.

"I'll tell him you'll be by later," Minnie went on, as if Thalia was still with her. "That's only forty minutes away. You can make that."

Thalia nodded again. Now that she was returning to normal, she seemed to have lost her words.

Minnie gave her a tender smile. "I've got to see to dinner, but you rest up." She stood and headed back to the kitchen area, muttering, "All the way from L.A. in one day!" and "That man…" as she went.

Thalia settled back into the chair, still sipping the tea. She knew she needed to be game-planning dinner with Bradley, but her brain was mushy.

She heard a door open. Men's voices filled the space. One was grumbling about the weather, but the other—Bradley's— said, "Minnie, what the hell is—"

Is she still doing here. That's what he was going to say. After all, he'd pretty much kicked her off his land, and now she was sitting in his house. He sounded none-too-happy about the whole prospect. How was she going to make it through dinner with him? She debated thanking Minnie for the tea and leaving, but then the smell of pot roast filled the air and Thalia realized that she hadn't eaten anything since she'd grabbed a sandwich in the airport. The Denver airport—eight hours ago.

"Now, now!" Thalia wasn't watching the conversation— listening was bad enough—but she could imagine Minnie waggling a finger at James Robert Bradley like he was a child and she was the boss. "You boys go on and get cleaned up. Dinner will be ready by and by."

"I don't want—"

"I said, go! Shoo!"

Thalia grinned in spite of herself at the mental image that filled out that conversation. The thought of Minnie, who was on the petite side of things and probably in her late forties, scolding James Robert Bradley was nothing short of hilarious.

She was safe, for now. Minnie was going to feed her and make sure she was warm. Thalia settled back into the comfy chair, her eyelids drooping as she watched the flames dance before her. She needed to figure out how to convince Bradley to listen to her without him throwing her out of the house. She needed a plan.

But first, she needed to rest. Just a little bit.

Two

J.R. was a grown man and, as such, did not stomp and pout when he didn't get his way. Instead, he grumbled. Loudly.

"This is my house, by God," he grumbled as he went up the back stairs.

"That it is," Hoss agreed behind him.

Hoss was always quick to agree when the facts were incontrovertible. "I'm the boss around here," J.R. added, more to himself than to his best friend.

"Most days," Hoss said with a snort.

J.R. shot the man a dirty look over his shoulder. "Every day," he said with more force than he needed. He was overreacting, but damn if that woman hadn't tripped every single alarm bell in his head.

They reached the second floor. Hoss's room was at the far end, Minnie's was in the middle across from two guest rooms that never saw a guest and J.R.'s was at the other.

"She don't look dangerous." Hoss scratched at his throat in his lazy way, which J.R. knew was entirely deceptive.

"Shows what you know," J.R. replied. He knew exactly how dangerous innocent-looking people—women—from Hollywood could be. "She's not to be trusted."

Damn, but he hated when Hoss gave him that look—the look that said he was being a first-class jerk. Rather than stand here in his chaps and argue the finer points of women, J.R. turned and walked—not stomped—down to his room.

He needed a hot shower in the worst way. His face was still half-frozen from riding out to check on the cattle and buffalo. He shut his bedroom door firmly—not slamming it—and began to strip off the layers. First went the long coat, then the chaps, then the jeans and sweater, followed by the two layers of long underwear and T-shirts. Despite being bundled up like a baby, he was still cold.

And that woman—the one sitting in *his* chair, in front of *his* fire—had shown up here in nothing but a skirt. And tights. And those boots, the ones that went almost up to her knees. "Stupid," he muttered to himself as he cranked his shower on high. What was she thinking, wearing next to nothing when the wind chill was somewhere around minus forty degrees below? She wasn't thinking, that's what. Hollywood types were notoriously myopic, and there was no doubt in J.R.'s mind that she was a Hollywood type.

The hot water rushed over him. J.R. bowed his head and let the water hit his shoulders. Against his will, his mind turned back to those boots, those tights. Those *legs*. Yeah, that woman clearly underestimated the force of winter in Montana. Probably thought that little coat was enough to keep her warm.

The moment he caught himself wondering what was under that coat, J.R. slammed on the brakes. He was not some green kid, distracted by a pretty face and a great body. No matter how blue her lips had been, that didn't make up for the fact that she'd come looking for James Robert Bradley. She wanted that name—the name J.R. had buried deep in Big Sky country eleven years ago. She wasn't here for him.

No one was ever here for him.

Except Minnie and Hoss, he reminded himself. They were his friends, his family and his crew all rolled into one. They knew who he really was, and that was good enough for him.

Warm and clean, he flipped off the water and rubbed down with the towel. He was going to fire Bernie. Hell, he should have fired the man years ago, but Bernie was his one thin link to his old life. He got J.R. some nice voice-over work and had, up until now, kept J.R.'s whereabouts to himself.

What had that woman dangled in front of Bernie's greedy little eyes to make him give her directions to the ranch? She had to be good at what she did. Not good enough to dress warmly, but J.R. knew that he could expect the full-court press from her for whatever she wanted James Robert Bradley to do.

He slid into a clean pair of jeans, making sure to put all the dirty things in the hamper. If he didn't, he'd have to listen to Minnie go on and on about *men* this and *men* that. It was easier to pick up after himself. Plus—not that he'd tell Minnie this—he preferred things neat. Clean.

Simple.

J.R. went to grab a shirt and paused. His hand was on his favorite flannel, the one he'd worn so much the collar was fraying. Minnie kept threatening to make a rag of it, but so far, she'd done no such thing.

Maybe he should put on something a little nicer. A little less tattered. He could clean up well, after all. Maybe he should…

Was he serious? Was he actually standing in his closet, debating what to wear because some uninvited, unwanted *female* had barged into his house? Was he hard up or what?

His brain, ever resourceful, rushed in to remind him it had been two years and seven months since his last failed

attempt at a relationship. Pretty much the textbook definition of hard up.

Didn't matter. She wasn't welcome here. And after he hu-
mored Minnie at dinner, he'd make sure she left his property
and never, ever came back. He grabbed his favorite shirt.
Frays be damned.

His resolve set, he shoved his feet into his house mocca-
sins and threw his door open.

And almost walked right into Minnie Red Horse.

"What?" he asked, so startled by the small woman that he
actually jumped back.

He didn't jump far enough, though. Minnie reached up
and poked him in the chest. "You listen to me, young man.
You *will* be nice and polite tonight."

Immediately, he went on the defensive. "Oh, it's my fault
she doesn't know it's winter out here?"

"I am ashamed to think that you left her out there in the
wind, J.R. I thought that you knew better than to treat a guest
like that."

He felt the hackles on the back of his neck go up. Minnie
had already busted out the big, shame-based guns. He'd be
lying if he said it didn't work—he hated to disappoint Minnie
in any way. But, he was a reformed actor. Lying used to be his
entire life. So he slapped on a stern look and glared at Minnie. "She's not a guest. She's a trespasser, Minnie. And if I
recall correctly, *you're* the one who shot at the last trespasser."

That had been the nail in the coffin of his last failed relationship. He'd been trying to decide if he loved Donna or not
when he'd invited her to spend the night at the ranch. Things
had been going fine until he took her up to his room. There,
she'd taken one look at James Robert Bradley's Oscar, his
photos, his life—and everything had changed. All she had
talked about was how he was really famous, and why on
earth hadn't he told her, and this was so amazing, that she
was here with him. Except she hadn't been. She'd thought

she was with James Robert. In the space of a minute, she'd forgotten that J.R. had even existed.

He'd broken up with her a few weeks later, and then, like clockwork, a few weeks after that, a man with an expensive camera had come snooping around. J.R. had been in the barn with Hoss when they'd heard the crunch of tires. J.R. had wanted to go out and confront the stranger, but Hoss had held him back. Rifle in hand, Minnie had been the one to claim that she'd never heard of anyone named Bradley, and if she saw that man again, she'd shoot him. Then she'd put a few bullets a few feet from the man, and that had been the end of that.

"That man was a parasite," Minnie said. "This is different. She's not like that."

"How would you know? She's here for James Robert. She wants something, Minnie. She'll ruin everything we've got, everything I've worked so hard for."

Minnie rolled her eyes. "Stop being so dramatic. Call it woman's intuition, or my Indian senses, my maternal instincts—whatever floats your boat. That woman is not a threat to you or any of us." She jabbed a finger back into J.R.'s chest. "And I expect you to be a gentleman. Do I make myself clear?"

"Don't tell me what to do, Minnie. You're not my—" Before the immature retort was all the way out, J.R. bit it back. Not soon enough, though.

A pained shadow crossed over Minnie's face, which made J.R. feel like the biggest jerk in the world. The fact was, Minnie had offered to adopt him a few years after they'd settled into the ranch. Oh, not the legal, court-based adoption—J.R. was a grown man—but she'd asked him if he wanted to be adopted into her family through the Lakota tribe. The fact was, she'd always been more of a mother to him than his own flesh-and-blood mother had ever been. The Red Horse family was his family. That was all there was to it.

J.R. had said no. He'd claimed he wasn't comfortable being a white man in an American Indian tribe, which was true. He knew that if word got out that James Robert Bradley had been adopted into a Lakota tribe, the storm of gossip would hurt everyone, not just him. And he couldn't hurt Minnie or Hoss.

Any more than he had. "I'm sorry," he offered. "It's just…"

Minnie patted his arm. "It's okay. You're a little… spooked."

"Yeah." Not that he'd want Hoss to know that, but Minnie and all of her womanly, Indian-y intuition already understood, so denying it was pointless. The woman downstairs had spooked him.

"Despite that, I expect both of my boys to be nice and polite." Her gaze flicked down over his frayed collar. "Respectable, even."

That was how fights with Minnie went. J.R. was the boss, but she was the mother. Forgiveness was quick and easy, not the dance of death it had been with Norma Bradley.

"I'm not taking the part. Whatever she wants, I'm not doing it."

"Did I say anything about that? No, I did not. All I said was that you were going to be a gentleman to our guest."

"Not my guest."

"Our visitor, then." Minnie looked like she wanted to poke him again, but she didn't. "Do it for me, J.R. Do you know how long it's been since we had a visitor out here? Months, that's how long. I want to talk to someone besides you two knuckleheads, and if it's a woman who's got the latest gossip? All the better."

J.R. sighed. Minnie had a huge weak spot for gossip. She subscribed to all the tabloids, read TMZ every day and probably knew more about the goings-on in the entertainment industry than he did. "One meal. Humor me. And don't worry, I wasn't going to ask her to stay, *despite* the fact that it's late and the winds are terrible."

He ignored the unveiled attempt at guilt. She was right. He owed her, and if that meant pretending they were having a girls-night-in for dinner, well, he'd suck it up. "That's good."

"I got her a room at Lloyd's." With that semidefiant statement, Minnie turned on her heel and headed back to her kitchen domain. "Dinner's in fifteen," she called back, loud enough that Hoss could hear her in his room.

Great, just great, J.R. thought as he hung his favorite shirt back up and pulled the green flannel Minnie had gotten him for Christmas off the hanger. Somehow, he knew that forty miles wasn't enough space between him and the woman from Hollywood.

A few minutes later, he headed down to the kitchen. Minnie was checking on something in the oven. "Tell her dinner's ready," she said without looking at him.

She was punishing him, pure and simple. Bad enough that he deserved it, but still.

J.R. headed down to his chair at the far end of the room. All he could see of the stranger was her golden hair peeking out from above the chair's back. The color was the kind of blond that spoke of sun-swept days at the beach, but he'd put money on it being fake.

Aw, hell. She was asleep. Slouched way down in the chair, Minnie's buffalo robe falling off her shoulders—her mouth open enough to make her look completely kissable. J.R. swallowed that observation back, but it wasn't easy. Her now-bootless legs were stretched out before her, and the patterned tights seemed to go on forever. Lord. Despite a second attempt at swallowing, his mouth had gone bone-dry. "Miss?"

She didn't move. Her head was resting on one hand; the other hand was wrapped around her waist. Minnie was right. The woman didn't look like she was capable of destroying his life.

Looks weren't everything, he reminded himself. He couldn't let his guard down. That thought, however, didn't stop him from sitting on his heels in front of her. Her hair had been slicked back into some fancy twist, but now parts of it had come loose, falling around her face in a way that was messy and beautiful at the same time. Some parts of him hadn't gotten the message, it seemed, because he wanted to do nothing more than brush that hair away from her face.

He didn't. Instead, he gave her shoulder a gentle shake before he jerked his hand back. As if a sleeping woman could bite him. "Miss, wake up."

She jolted, her eyelids fluttering open. J.R. braced himself for the reaction when she realized he was close enough to trap. Would she immediately launch into her pitch or go for cloying flattery?

When her eyes focused on him, a small smile curved the corners of her mouth. *Here it comes,* J.R. thought.

"It's *you*," she breathed. The warm glow in her eyes didn't seem connected to the fire behind him, and the soft adoration in her voice should have grated on his every nerve. But it didn't.

"Yup. It's me." Which felt weirdly personal, because he knew she wasn't here for him, but for the man he used to be.

Then time froze—absolutely froze—as he watched her stretch out a hand and trace the tips of her fingers down his cheek and over his ten-day-old beard. The touch was way more than weirdly personal—it was downright, damnably erotic. The sudden shift of blood from his brain to other parts made him almost dizzy. Hell, yeah, she'd look this good waking up in his bed, and if he had her there, he would be damn sure it wouldn't stop with a little pat on the cheek.

What the hell was he thinking?

That was the problem. He wasn't.

He must have pulled back without realizing it, because she dropped her hand and blinked a whole bunch more. "Oh. *Oh,*" she said, and he could see the consciousness dawning. "Um…"

Desperate to put a little more space between him and this woman who had spooked him in more ways than one, J.R. stood up and back. "Dinner's ready," he added, because that was the safest thing to say. Also, the most honest.

The woman dropped her eyes, warmth racing across her cheeks. Did she feel the same confusion he did? *Don't flatter yourself,* he thought. Of course she was confused. He'd woken her up from a dead sleep. She had a good excuse to feel a little lost right now.

He didn't.

She smoothed her hair back, but several of the locks refused to stay. "I had some boots," she said. All the softness was gone from her voice now, and she sounded more like the woman who had barged into his life.

"Right here." He picked up her boots from where Minnie had propped them by the fire and handed them to her.

She made sure not to touch him when she took them. And he should not have been disappointed by that. "Is there... I need to wash up..."

Women in general—and this woman in particular—should not look quite so innocent when they blushed. "Sure." He pointed to the bathroom that was behind her.

She turned, but then stopped. "Should I leave *this* here?" She motioned to the robe.

The way she said *this* made it clear that she wasn't sure she trusted it. "Minnie's buffalo robe? Yeah, that's fine."

"Oh. A buffalo robe." Some of her blush disappeared as she paled. What did she think it was? Maybe she was one of those strident vegetarians. Instead of launching into an animal-rights lecture, she put on a weak smile and said, "Okay, thanks," before she went to the bathroom.

Well, if that didn't beat all. Where was the full-court press? Where were the obnoxious compliments designed to sway his ego? Nowhere. All he got was someone who, for a sleepy second, looked happy to see him.

Dinner was a huge mistake. He debated hiding in his room until the woman—whose name he still did not know—left. Then he caught Minnie giving him a wallop of a glare from the other side of the room as she tapped a wooden spoon on the counter. Right, right. He'd promised to be nice and polite, which probably didn't include hiding.

So he set the table instead. Hoss finally clumped down the stairs, just as J.R. was finishing. For a man who wasn't afraid of putting in a hard day's work on the range, Hoss had the unique ability to never be present when a small household chore needed to be done. "Well?"

Minnie flashed her wooden spoon like it was a weapon. "She's staying for dinner, and you will behave or else."

"When am I not a perfect angel?" Hoss gave her his best puppy eyes, but it didn't work. "Can I at least sit by her?"

"No." J.R. didn't mean to sound so possessive; it burst out of him.

Minnie shot him a funny look. "No, I'm going to sit by her. You two are going to sit in your normal spots and keep your hands, feet and all other objects to yourself. Clear?"

Hoss met J.R.'s gaze and lifted one eyebrow, as if to say, *game on.* Jeez, if Hoss was acting this much the cad now, how much of a pain would he become when he saw her all warmed up? "Yes, ma'am."

Then a noise at the other end of the room drew their attention. The woman was standing by the chair now, her hair fixed, her boots on and her coat off. Whoa. The gray wool dress she had on was cut close, revealing a knockout figure that went with her knockout legs. Either she was stunning—hell, she *was* stunning—or she'd had a good plastic surgeon. One never could be sure when it came to Hollywood types.

Then her gaze locked on to his, and he swore he felt the same dizzy charge that he'd felt when she'd touched him, only this time, there was a clear thirty feet of space between them.

She's not here for you, J.R. practically shouted at himself. *She's here for James Robert.*

Damn shame she wasn't there for him, though.

"Whoa," Hoss muttered next to him, and Minnie promptly smacked his butt with the spoon. "Ow!"

"Feeling better?" Minnie pushed past J.R. and went to greet her visitor.

"Much, thanks." The woman gave Minnie a friendly smile. "Where should I put my coat?"

"Lay it on the chair. I'll make the introductions." Minnie took her by the arm and led her to where J.R. and Hoss were gaping like horny seventh graders. "This is Hoss Red Horse, and J. R. Bradley."

J.R. rolled his eyes—obviously the woman knew who he was. Otherwise, she wouldn't be here.

"Boys," Minnie went on, giving them both the warning stink eye, "this is Thalia Thorne."

Hoss stuck out his hand. "A pleasure, Ms. Thorne." Miracle of miracles, that was all he said.

"Nice to meet you…Hoss." She looked from him to Minnie. "Are you two related?"

Hoss's polite grin dialed right over into trouble. "Yeah, but she don't like people to know I'm her son. Makes her feel old or something."

Minnie hit him with the spoon again, which caused Thalia to stifle a giggle. Her eyes still laughed, though.

Not that J.R. was staring or anything.

Then those eyes—a clear, deep blue—shifted to him, and she held out her hand. "It's nice to meet you, J.R."

He couldn't do anything but stare at her. She wasn't going to insist on calling him James Robert? Just like that?

Minnie cleared her throat and shot him a dangerous glare. Right. Acknowledging that she'd spoken to him was probably the nice, polite thing to do. "Likewise, Thalia." Against his better judgment, he took her hand in his and gave it a gentle squeeze. Heat flowed between them. Probably because she'd warmed up in front of the fire. Yeah, that was it.

That small, curved smile danced over her nice lips and was then gone. "Dinner smells wonderful, Minnie. I can't remember the last time I had a home-cooked meal."

There was the flattery, and boy, was it working on Minnie. She blushed and grinned and shooed all of them to the table, saying, "Sit by me, dear, so we can talk."

Of course, sitting by Minnie also turned out to be sitting by J.R., as Thalia was on the corner between him and Minnie. His thoughts immediately turned to the patterned tights under the table—and their close proximity to his own legs— way more than they should have. Man, he was hard up.

How the hell was he going to make it through dinner?

Three

"So, tell us about yourself," Minnie said to Thalia as she passed a basket of piping hot corn muffins around the table.

J.R. waited. Everyone waited, including Hoss, which was saying something. Hoss wasn't seriously trying to make a move on this woman, was he? In front of his own mother? Ugh. This whole thing couldn't be more awkward, J.R. decided.

"I'm an associate producer." J.R. couldn't help but notice she looked at Hoss and Minnie—but not at him. "I work for Bob Levinson at Halcyon Pictures."

"He's an ass." The moment the words left his mouth, Minnie looked like she would smack him upside the head with the spoon—if only their "visitor" wasn't sitting in between the two of them. "Pardon my language."

One of those quick, nervous smiles darted over Thalia's face. But she still didn't quite meet his eyes. The closest she got was more in the region of his shoulder. What the hell kind of new negotiating tactic was this—ignore the person you were trying to ensnare? "It's true he has a certain reputation."

A certain reputation? J.R. had had the intense displeasure of working on two Levinson movies—*Colors That Run* and *The Cherry Trees*—and both had been sheer torture tests. On his good days, Levinson had been demeaning and derogatory. On his worst days, he had inspired J.R. to envision creative ways to off the man. He couldn't imagine Levinson had mellowed with age. His kind never did. They just got more and more caustic, leaving nothing but scorched earth behind them.

And, in Levinson's case, a growing list of Oscar winners. He was an ass, all right, but because he delivered the box office returns and the shiny little gold men, everyone in Hollywood gave him a free pass. Except J.R., who wasn't in Hollywood anymore.

And this Thalia—who looked soft and could pull off innocent—worked directly for him. In so many ways, she was not trustworthy.

"Are you famous?" Hoss asked.

J.R. shot Hoss a dirty look, which earned him a grin that bordered on predatory. Did Hoss think he had a shot? Hell, no.

Thalia's laugh was small but polite. "Only to my mother. Every time one of my movies comes to Norman, Oklahoma, she rounds up a bunch of friends." Hints of color graced her cheeks, but she showed no other sign of being embarrassed by this. "They sit through the credits and when my name rolls by, they all stand and cheer. And I'm famous for a whole three minutes."

"So you're not originally from California?" Minnie's eyes were bright and her smile was huge. She was having fun, J.R. realized. That made him feel better. Not much, but a little.

"No, I've only been there for about ten years."

"What does an associate producer do?" Hoss was nailing nice and polite right out of the gate, which only made J.R. look worse. When Hoss was rewarded with a nice smile, J.R.

had to fight the urge to kick him under the table. Hoss was not her type. True, J.R. didn't know exactly what her type was, but Hoss was a decent, honest, hardworking fellow, even if he was a bit of a joker. In other words, he was the kind of man that women like Thalia Thorne probably ate for breakfast.

"A little bit of everything. I scout locations, arrange funding and hire talent." She managed to say that entire line without looking at J.R. The amount of effort she put into *not* looking at him broadcast that she knew he was here, loud and clear.

"I was in a movie once." J.R. fought the urge to roll his eyes. "Me and Minnie, we were extra Native Americans in *Hell for Leather.*" Hoss shook his head in mock sadness. "First, I got killed, then they cut my part. That's why I gave up Hollywood and stuck to ranching, you know."

What a load of crap. Mostly true crap—everything except that last line, which J.R. took as a personal attack. He was about to punch Hoss in the arm when Thalia giggled. "Is that so? Fame can be fickle like that."

"Sure can." Hoss shot him a look that said one thing, and one thing only—*I'm winning.* "Were you always a producer?"

"Not originally. I wanted to be an actress." Thalia's voice got that soft quality again. "I came close—I had a three-episode arc on *Alias*—that girl-next-door-superspy show." Then her eyes brightened and she gave Hoss a grin that said she was in on the joke. "I got killed, too. It's murder on one's career to be dying all the time."

A former actress? Another strike against her—or it should have been. The way she'd said it felt like she'd plucked a single string somewhere inside J.R. and that string hummed in recognition.

So what? Hollywood was the land of broken dreams. He would not be swayed by a calculated play on his sympathies.

"Do you know that Jennifer Garner?" When Thalia nodded, Minnie's eyes lit up. "I always wondered if she was a nice person or if she'd kill you."

"She's normal—but the baby showers! You should have seen the gifts!" As Thalia revealed all sorts of firsthand details and Minnie ate it up, J.R. noticed that everything she said was warm and friendly. Nothing malicious passed her lips.

Not that he was thinking about her lips. That wasn't it at all.

No, he was thinking Minnie's sixth sense might be right— Thalia Thorne didn't act like someone who'd come digging for dirt. But she'd come for something. *What* was the question. He knew it was only a matter of time before she got around to it.

She didn't seem in a hurry, though. Instead, she ate and talked like they were all the oldest of friends while Minnie passed around the pot roast and the potatoes. They were J.R.'s favorite kind, smashed red potatoes with rosemary and garlic, but tonight, nothing tasted good. To him, anyway. Thalia sat there oohing and aahing over everything, and Minnie looked like she'd hit the jackpot. Lord, it was irritating. It was almost as if he wasn't even sitting at the table.

"So, what brings you out our way?" Minnie kept her tone light and friendly, but there was no mistaking that this was *the* question on everyone's mind. Including J.R.'s.

Her gaze cast down, Thalia wiped her mouth with her napkin. For a second, J.R. almost felt sorry for her. So far, she hadn't done a single thing he'd expected of her, and he got the sense that she knew exactly how far she'd overreached.

Then she squared her shoulders. "I'm working on a movie tentatively titled *Blood for Roses*. It's slated to be released next December."

Just in time to be considered for Levinson's required slew of Oscars, no doubt. "What's it about?" Hoss was now leaning forward, eyes on Thalia as if every word that fell from her mouth was a ruby.

"It's a Western set in Kansas after the Civil War. A family of freed slaves tries to start a new life, but some of the locals aren't too keen on the idea." She cleared her throat. This was the pitch, no doubt, but she came off as hesitant to make it. Like she knew that J.R. was going to throw her out, and she didn't want to go yet. "Eastwood is attached to direct, Freeman has signed on and we're in talks with Denzel."

It was an impressive roster. No doubt Levinson was hoping to break nomination records.

"Oh, I love Denzel, especially when he's playing the bad guy." Thalia had Minnie already, that much was clear. "Have you met him? Is he as sexy in real life as he is in the movies?"

"It's not quite the same," Thalia admitted, "although he is quite good-looking." She shrugged. "When you're around famous people long enough, you stop worrying so much about who's the most famous or who's the hottest. Sooner or later, it has to come down to whether or not they're someone you can work with." This blanket statement that could only be described as reasonable hung out there before she added, "Having said that, Denzel is someone that almost everyone enjoys working with, and his wife is lovely."

Then she looked at him. Not the kind of look that asked if he'd bought what she was selling, but the kind of look that seemed to be asking for understanding.

What the hell was this?

"So what part did you have in mind for him?" Hoss jerked his chin toward J.R. with all the subtlety of a dead skunk in the middle of the road.

She favored J.R. with another look that was lost in the no-man's-land of apologetic and sympathetic. It made her look vulnerable, honest even—which was completely disarming. He didn't like that look or how it plucked at those strings inside him, not one bit. "I thought James Robert Bradley would be perfect for the role of Sean Bridger, the grizzled Confederate Civil War vet who unexpectedly finds himself helping defend the freedmen's land." Her face was almost unreadable, but he could see the pulse at the base of her neck pounding. "I wanted to see if you'd be interested in the part, J.R."

Getting him signed on was her idea, not Levinson's? Wait. There was something more to what she'd said. He scrambled to replay it while keeping his own face blank. She'd thought James Robert was perfect—but she'd asked *him,* J.R., if he was interested. Her gaze held tight to his, and he felt that flow of energy between them again. She'd been right to avoid looking at him before—he could get all kinds of lost in her ice-blue eyes. Because now she was not just looking at him, but into him, through all the walls he'd thrown up between James Robert Bradley and J.R. That's why she wasn't doing the full-court press. She understood the difference between his two lives. Understood it, and possibly even respected it.

She was more dangerous than he'd thought possible.

Eastwood to direct. Freeman and Washington to star. The who's who of people who could pull off a Western—and she'd thought of him. He'd be lying if he said he wasn't flattered, but that didn't change things. "I'm not interested."

Not in the part, anyway. He managed to break eye contact, which snapped the tension between them.

"Any Indians in this movie?" For once, J.R. didn't want Hoss to shut up. It'd be better for everyone if Hoss did all the talking.

She was silent for two beats too long. He shouldn't care that he'd disappointed her, so he ignored the inconvenient emotion.

"Sadly, no. I believe they were all pushed off the land before our story begins. If something opens up, I'll be sure to keep you in mind."

Conversation seemed to die after that, as if no one knew what was supposed to be said next. J.R. wanted her to leave and take this discomfort with her. He didn't want her to look at him—through him—anymore. He didn't want to think about her pretty eyes or long legs, and he sure as hell didn't want her to give him another just-woke-up, so-glad-to-see-you look of longing. And if she wouldn't leave, he had a good mind to bail.

But he'd promised Minnie to be polite. So he focused on eating the food that was tasteless. After a few moments, Minnie asked another question about some actor, and Thalia responded with what felt like a little too much forced enthusiasm.

"Now, I've got a chocolate cake or there's blondies," Minnie said, which meant J.R. was almost free.

"Oh, thank you so much, but I need to get on the road." Thalia glanced at him and added, "This has been wonderful, and you've been more than kind, but I couldn't possibly take up any more of your time."

"At least take some of the blondies. I insist." Minnie was up and moving. She never let anyone leave without an extra meal.

"I'll get the dishes." Hoss started clearing the table, which wasn't like him at all.

Before J.R. could process Hoss's sudden reversal of his no-housework policy, he found himself sitting alone with Thalia. It's not that he was afraid to look at her, afraid to feel the way her presence pulled on parts of him he pretended he'd forgotten existed. Wasn't that at all. He didn't want to give her another chance to make her case. He didn't want to tell her no again. He'd already done it twice. Once should have been enough.

Nice. Polite. He could feel Minnie's eyes boring a hole in the back of his head. What the hell? He'd never see her again anyway. "What are you going to tell Levinson?"

"I'm not sure." Out of the corner of his eye, he could see her eyebrows knot together. She looked worried. For some reason, that bothered him.

"You seem like..." Aw, hell. Was he about to pay her a

compliment? "You seem like a nice person. What are you doing working for *him?*"

Her gaze locked on to his, and that connection he didn't want to feel was right there, pulling on him more and more. "I've found that life often takes you places you'd never thought you'd go."

She was doing it again, looking right into him. So what if what she said made all kinds of sense? So what if she came off as decent? So what if she was completely at ease with Minnie and Hoss?

She didn't belong here. She might well go back and tell Levinson all sorts of fabricated crap. He might find himself on the cover of next week's *Star,* and he might find more people freezing to death on his property, trying to snap a picture of the elusive James Robert Bradley.

"Here we are." *Saved by dessert,* J.R. thought as Minnie bustled up to the table. "Now don't try to get to Billings tonight. Here's directions to Lloyd's place. I'll call him and let him know you're on your way. And our number's here—" she tapped on the paper "—so call me when you get there."

J.R. cleared his throat in the most menacing way possible. Minnie was giving out their number? When did that become a good idea? Never, that's when.

"I want to make sure you get there, safe and sound." Minnie said the words to Thalia, but she shot the look of death at J.R.

Thalia didn't acknowledge his rudeness. Instead, she thanked Minnie and Hoss with such warmth that it felt like they were all old friends. Hoss got her coat and, doing his best impersonation of a gentleman, held it for her.

After Thalia buttoned up, she turned to face him. J.R. was torn between not looking at her so she'd leave faster and looking at her good and long. He wasn't going to see her again, and he certainly didn't want to, but he knew that the memory of her strange visit would haunt him for a long time after she left. He wanted to make sure he remembered her as she was.

"J.R." That was all she said as she extended her hand.

He shouldn't shake—for his own sanity if nothing else—but if he didn't, Minnie might stop feeding him. *Suck it up,* he thought. So what if she was maybe the only other woman on the planet—besides Minnie—to call him J.R. after she knew about James Robert? Didn't matter. She was leaving and that was that. "Thalia."

Her skin was soft and much warmer now. A look crossed her face, almost the same as the one she'd given him when he woke her up earlier—except she was wide awake now. That look was going to stay with him. He wanted to be annoyed with it, and with her, but he couldn't be.

"It's been such a pleasure meeting you." When Minnie started talking, Thalia let go of his hand. "You're welcome back anytime, Thalia."

Everyone paused, like they were waiting for him to say something gruff or rude, but J.R. held his tongue. Part of him wanted to see her again, to see if she was really like this, or if the whole evening had been an elaborate act designed to lull him into complacency.

He wanted to see if she'd still look at him like that. *Into* him, like that.

Minnie walked her to her car. Hoss watched them from the front window. But J.R. stood rooted to the spot.

He wanted to see her again.

He hoped like hell he never did.

Four

Billings hadn't gotten any closer overnight, Thalia realized as she drove to the airport the next morning. Five hours was a lot of time to think. Maybe too much time.

"What are you going to tell Levinson?" J.R. had asked and she still didn't have an answer. The night of dreamless sleep in a room that hadn't been touched since the days of *The Brady Bunch* and a breakfast of bacon, eggs and extra-strong black coffee with Lloyd hadn't gotten her any closer to a plan.

What were her options? She could quit before Levinson had a chance to fire her. That might help her reputation in the short-term, but sooner or later the rumor mill would start grinding again. People would dig up the old news and the old photos of her and Levinson and start asking if maybe another affair had led to her sudden departure. It wouldn't matter that there was no affair this time. Just the suggestion of one would be damaging enough—for her. For the second time, Levinson would come out unscathed and Thalia's career would be ground into a pulp. And like the last time, when no one had hired her as an actress, this time no one would hire her as a producer. And if you weren't an actor and you weren't a producer, then you weren't anybody in Hollywood.

She needed to avoid any action that had a hint of juicy gossip. So quitting was out. What could she do to keep her job? She could present Levinson with a list of reasons why Bradley had been a bad idea—*her* bad idea. Except that any reasons she came up with would pretty much have to be bold-faced lies. The man had been everything she'd hoped to find. He was less gorgeous than he'd been fifteen years ago—less polished, less perfect. He was less the pretty boy now.

No, he wasn't pretty. *Handsome.* His hair had deepened from golden-boy blond to the kind of brown that only reflected hints of gold in the firelight. His ten-day-old beard made it clear he wasn't a boy anymore. He'd put on weight, maybe thirty pounds, but instead of going right to his gut, as often happened when actors let themselves go, it seemed like he'd added an all-over layer of muscle. And not the kind that came from hours spent at a gym. No, the way his body had moved, from the way he rode his horse to the way he had sat on his heels in front of her spoke of nothing but hard-earned strength.

All of those things were swoon-worthy, but his amber eyes—those were what held Thalia's attention. They were the only things that hadn't changed. No, that wasn't true, either. They looked the same, but to Thalia, it seemed like there'd been more going on beyond the lovely color. And for one sweet, confused moment, she thought she'd been privy to what he was thinking.

She mentally slapped her head again. Had she touched that beard? Had she acted like a lovesick schoolgirl, swooning over the biggest hunk in the world? Yes, she had. And why? Because when she'd opened her eyes, she'd thought she'd still been dreaming. How else to explain the small smile he'd given her—*her,* of all people. She'd been dreaming, all right.

Neither part of him—James Robert the superstar or J.R. the reclusive rancher—would be the least bit welcoming to the likes of her. She felt like a fool. She'd embarrassed herself and, based on his behavior during the meal, she'd embarrassed him, too.

At least she thought she had. The exchange—the touch, the smile—between them couldn't have taken more than twenty seconds. J. R. Bradley was hard to read. She could see so much churning behind his eyes, but she couldn't make sense of it. She had no good idea if he'd been embarrassed, flattered or offended. Or all three. All she knew was that her little slipup had had some sort of effect on him. The other thing she knew was that J.R.'s eyes were dangerous. Looking into those liquid pools of amber was a surefire way to make another mistake.

Thalia shook her head, trying to forget the way his stubble had pricked at her fingers. She could relive that moment again when she had the time—all the time in the world, if she was going to be unemployed. Quitting wasn't the best option. Lying about J.R. was out. Anything she said would take on a life of its own, and she had the awful feeling that if she started the rumor mill churning about him, he might trample her next time. What could she do to save her job?

She was walking into Billings Airport when she realized that she only had two options. One was to present Levinson with a list of better-suited actors to take the role and hope that he wouldn't ask questions about what had happened with Bradley. Which was asking a lot of hope. It had taken a great deal of negotiating to convince Levinson that Bradley was perfect for the role. It would take a heck of a lot more to convince him Bradley wasn't.

The other choice was to go back and get Bradley.

"May I help you?"

Thalia realized she was standing in front of the check-in desk, her return ticket in one hand.

She *had* to get Bradley. She couldn't give up on him. He wouldn't be happy to see her again—at least, she didn't think he would be—but Minnie Red Horse was another matter entirely. Thalia did have an open invitation to come back to the Bar B Ranch, after all. If she didn't take advantage of that, did she deserve to keep her job?

"Ma'am? May I help you?" The clerk at the check-in desk was beginning to get worried.

Thalia couldn't leave. But she wasn't prepared to stay. She'd planned for a quick overnight trip. She had her makeup and meds, her laptop and a change of underwear. Her dress and coat had already proven to be woefully inadequate. If she was going back out to the Bar B, she needed to be ready this time.

"Yes," she finally said as she advanced to the desk. The clerk looked relieved that Thalia wasn't some weirdo flaking out. "I need to buy some clothes. Where's a good place to shop here?"

The clerk went right back over to worried. "The Rimrock mall has a J.C. Penney."

It had been ages since she'd been in the kind of mall that had a J.C. Penney—not since she had been back in Oklahoma. It seemed fitting—and would probably cost her a fourth of what stuff in Hollywood would. She could absorb a little wardrobe adjustment, especially if it kept her employed. "Perfect."

Thalia got directions, made sure her open-end ticket was still open and then re-rented the car. She called Lloyd to tell him that she'd be back tonight, and if it was okay with him, she'd probably be staying a few nights more.

Then she went shopping.

J.R. was getting sick of winter. Another day of riding out on the range to make sure that the cattle and buffalo had open water, and another day of trucking hay out to the far reaches of the ranch for wild mustangs they pastured. The chores didn't bother him—it was the bone-chilling cold that hurt more every day, and they hadn't even had a big winter storm yet. Which was another source of worry. If it didn't start snowing a little more, the ranch would be low on water for the coming summer. If it snowed too much, he'd lose some cattle.

"Getting too old for this," Hoss muttered off to his side.

"You're only thirty," J.R. reminded him. "Many happy years of winter ranching ahead of you."

"Hell," Hoss said as a gust of wind smacked them in the face. "At least you have options. I'm stuck out here."

"Options? What are you talking about?"

Hoss turned in the saddle, holding his hat to shield his face from the wind. "You could have gone to California, you know. You didn't have to stay out here with me and Minnie."

"Didn't want to." He was surprised at how much that statement felt like a lie.

"Man, why not? Pretty woman like that offers to give you money for nothing to go where the sun is shining? Shoot. I'd have gone."

J.R. chose not to respond to this. It had been two days since Thalia Thorne had shown up. On the surface, nothing had changed. He was still the boss, cattle still had to be watered and it was still cold. But something felt different. Minnie had been quiet after their visitor had left—not happy, like J.R. had hoped she'd be. But she hadn't scolded him on his lousy behavior. She hadn't said anything, which wasn't like her. And now Hoss was laying into him.

He saw the something that was different as soon as they crested the last hill between them and the ranch house J.R. had built a year after he'd bought the place. There, in the drive, was a too-familiar car.

"Would you look at that," Hoss mused, suddenly sounding anything but grumpy. "Looks like we got ourselves a pretty guest again."

"What is she doing here?"

Hoss shot him a look full of humor. "If you ain't figured that one out yet, I'm not gonna be the one to break it to you." Then he kicked his horse into a slow canter down to the barn.

Damn. And damn again. If he weren't so cold, he'd turn his horse around and disappear into the backcountry. Thalia Thorne might be able to find the ranch house, but she wouldn't survive the open range, not in her sexy little boots and tight dress.

The fact of the matter was, he was frozen. "She better not be in my chair again," he grumbled to himself as he rode toward the barn.

Hoss whistled as he unsaddled his horse. The sound grated on J.R.'s nerves something fierce. "Knock it off. She's not here for you."

"And you know that for sure, huh?" Hoss snorted. "She came for the shiny gold man in your lair up there—but that don't mean she won't stay for a little piece of Hoss."

J.R. felt his hands clench into fists. One of the things that had always made him and Hoss such fast friends had been that they didn't argue over women. Hoss went for the kind of bubbly, good-time gal that always struck J.R. as flighty, while he preferred women who could string together more than two coherent, grammatically correct sentences at a time. In the eleven years he'd been out here, he and Hoss had never once sparred over a woman.

There was a first for everything, apparently.

"She's off-limits." The words came out as more of a growl than a statement.

"Yeah?" Hoss puffed out his chest and met J.R.'s mean stare head-on. "I don't see you doing a bang-up job of getting her into your bed. If you aren't up to the task, maybe you should stand aside, *old* man."

J.R. bristled. He was only six years older than Hoss. The idiot was intentionally trying to yank his chain, and he was doing a damn fine job of it. J.R. did his best to keep his voice calm. As much as Thalia's reappearance pissed him off, he still didn't want to walk into the kitchen with a black eye or a busted nose. "I don't want her in my bed." Hoss snorted in disbelief, but J.R. chose to ignore him. "I don't want her in my house. And the more you make googly eyes at her, the more Minnie gushes at her, the more she'll keep coming back. She doesn't belong here."

Hoss didn't back down. But he didn't push it, either. Instead, he turned and headed for the house at a leisurely mosey, still whistling. Still planning on making a move on Thalia Thorne.

Cursing under his breath, J.R. groomed his horse at double-time speed. He did *not* want Thalia in his bed, no matter what Hoss said. She represented too big a threat to his life out here, the life he'd chosen. The fact that she was here again should be a big, honking sign to everyone that she was not to be taken lightly.

So why was he the only one alarmed? And why, for the love of everything holy, was his brain now imagining what she'd look like in his bed?

He tried to block out the images that filed through his mind in rapid succession—Thalia wrapped in the sheets, her hair tousled and loose, her shoulders bare, her *everything* bare. Waking her up with a kiss, seeing the way she gazed at him, feeling the way her body warmed to his touch...

J.R. groaned in frustration and kicked a hay bale as he headed toward the house. When had this become a problem? When had he let a woman get under his skin like this—a woman he didn't even *like?* When had his body started overruling his common sense, his self-preservation?

And when had Hoss decided a woman was more important than their friendship?

His mood did not improve when he walked into *his* kitchen to find Thalia, sitting on *his* stool, leaning into a hug with Hoss. That did it. J.R. was going to have to kill his best friend.

He must have growled, because Hoss shot him a look that said *I got here first* and Thalia sat up straight. The way her cheeks blushed a pale pink did not improve J.R.'s situation one bit.

"J.R., look who's back!" Hoss's tone of voice made it plenty clear that he was going to keep pushing J.R.'s buttons. His arm was still slung around her shoulders. "I was telling Thalia how good it was to see her pretty face again." The SOB then gave her another big squeeze. "You found a casting couch for me yet?"

Thalia laughed nervously as she pulled away from Hoss's embrace. "Sadly, I haven't found the couch that can handle you, Hoss. But I'll keep looking."

Then she turned her bright eyes to him. "Hello, J.R." She made no move to get up, no move to shake his hand—much less hug him. He wouldn't have trusted her if she had, but damned if it didn't piss him off all over again that she didn't.

Behind the Thalia and Hoss tableau, Minnie tapped her big wooden spoon on the counter as she looked daggers at him. *Be nice,* her eyes told him. Why was it his job to make nice when everyone else was flaunting his rules in his house? Screw it. Without a word, he turned away from the interloper and the two traitors and walked—not stomped—upstairs. He heard Hoss coming up behind him, but he didn't wait.

The shower did little to improve his mood, mostly because he couldn't stop thinking about that woman. At least this time, she was dressed appropriately. A cowl-neck sweater in an ice-blue color that matched her eyes had clung to her curves, revealing as much—if not more—than the short dress. Instead of those teasing tights, she was wearing jeans that hugged every inch of her long legs. And instead of delicate stilettos, she had on a pair of real cowboy boots. Her hair had been freed of the severe twist so that now it fell in loose waves around her face and shoulders.

She looked like someone who did, in fact, fit out here. Worse than that? She looked like she *belonged* out here.

It's a costume, he reminded himself as he rubbed dry with more force than normal. That wasn't the real her. He didn't know what the real her looked like, but it couldn't be that cowboy's dream come true down there.

If Hoss touched her again, J.R. would have to kill him.

He almost put on his favorite frayed shirt in protest of this whole ridiculous situation, but he couldn't pull the trigger. He went with the sweater Minnie had knit him two years ago for Christmas. It usually made her happy when he wore it. Clearly, it was his only hope of keeping her on his side right now.

He could do this. He wouldn't lose his temper, and he wouldn't add fuel to the fire. If need be, he wouldn't say anything. If he didn't engage, sooner or later Thalia Thorne would get tired of asking. It was that simple.

The glint of sunlight off gold slowed him up, and he found himself staring at his Oscar. He didn't know why he kept the damn thing out—after all, his Golden Globe and all his other awards were in a box in the back of his closet. Oscar had brought him nothing but heartache, today included. He hefted it off the mantle, feeling the cold metal. He'd been terrified the night he'd won, hoping and praying someone else—anyone else—would win, but knowing that the race was his to lose. And when they called his name, the terror had spiked right on over to panic. If he hadn't figured it out before that moment, he knew then that he'd lost any semblance of control he'd had over his life. People had always expected things of him—his mother, his agent, film people—but he'd known when he'd won that the life he'd barely managed to keep a grip on was going to be wrenched from his control.

And he'd been right. He'd stopped being a person and become nothing but a commodity.

He'd hated feeling powerless then, and he hated it now. That was the problem with Thalia Thorne. Her unwelcome intrusion left him feeling like he wasn't in control anymore.

He looked Oscar in the face. "I'm the boss around here," he said, more to himself than the inanimate object. So that woman had him a little spooked. So she'd won over Minnie and Hoss. He was not about to cede control of his life to the likes of her and, by extension, Levinson. No pretty face, no sweet touch and no amount of money would change his mind.

His resolve set, he headed downstairs. Nice? Sure. Polite? Barely. But he wasn't taking the part. He wasn't taking anything from Thalia Thorne.

At least he'd gotten back down to the kitchen before Hoss. Thalia was still on the stool with Minnie standing next to her. From the look of it, they were poring over Minnie's latest *People* magazine.

"I love this dress on Charlize," Minnie was saying in a wistful tone that was far more girlish than normal.

"Really? I thought the one she wore at last year's BAFTAs was better." Thalia glanced up at him, and damned if her face didn't light up almost exactly like it had when he'd woken her up two days ago.

He was *not* being swayed by her face. So he crossed his arms and glared at her. It didn't have the desired impact. Instead of paling or shrinking away, she favored him with a small grin. Damn.

"The BAFTAs?" Minnie was thankfully too engrossed in her fashion daydreams to notice his lack of manners.

"The British equivalent of the Oscars."

"Oh." It was hard to begrudge Minnie this little bit of fun, because she was clearly in seventh heaven. "Would pictures of that be online? We could look them up!"

"Sure." Although Thalia was talking to Minnie, she was

still looking at him like she was happy to see him again. For completely stupid reasons, J.R. was happy to note that she didn't look at Hoss like that. Just him.

"I'll go get my laptop." Minnie looked up, registering his presence for the first time. "Oh, J.R., keep an eye on the casserole, okay?"

"I'll do it," Thalia volunteered as Minnie all but ran up the back stairs to get her computer.

He was alone with Thalia. That realization left him with an uncomfortable pit in his stomach. This was his chance—maybe his only chance—to tell her off. He was tired of feeling out of place in his own home. It was time to return the favor.

When she swung those long legs off the stool to head toward the oven, he made his move. He grabbed her arm so hard that she spun into his chest with a squeak. And just like that, they were face-to-face, chest-to-chest.

Big, huge mistake. Her breasts pressed against his chest with little regard to the two layers of sweaters that stood between them. With her boots on, her face was only a few inches below his, and when she looked up into his eyes, he realized how little space separated his mouth from hers.

"What are you doing here?" Besides driving him to distraction, that was. His body strained to respond to the light scent of strawberries that hung around her. She smelled good enough to eat.

Down, boy.

"I came back to see Minnie." Her voice trembled a little as she pushed on his chest with her hands. Not hard—not enough to drive them apart—but enough to make him loosen his grip.

"It won't work."

"What won't?" She had the nerve to look innocent. That made him mad again, which distracted him from the pressure building behind his jeans' zipper.

"You're trying to get Minnie to convince me to take the part. It won't work."

He had her full attention—and that was becoming a problem. Her eyes were wide open, her lips were barely parted. All he'd have to do would be to lower his head without letting go of her. Did she taste as sweet as she smelled?

She angled her head to one side a little. Her hair tipped off her shoulders, exposing the curve of her neck. Her hands, which had been flat on his chest, curved at the fingers, as if she was trying to hold on to him, trying to pull him in closer.

Against his every wish, his head began to dip. He could not kiss her; he could not be turned on by her; he could *not* be interested in her—but he was. She was going to ruin the life he'd made, and he almost didn't care. It was almost worth the way she looked at him, soft and innocent and waiting to be kissed.

Almost.

"Did Levinson tell you to seduce me? Is that it?"

Indignant color flooded her cheeks as everything inviting about her burned up in the heat of her glare. J.R. wasn't all that surprised when she pushed him back and slapped his face all at once. "I'm not his whore." Her voice was level, cold— as if she were in complete control of the situation.

The way she hissed the words made it pretty clear that J.R. had finally, *finally* gotten under her skin. And it was still possible that her fury was an act, a cover for a seduction gone wrong.

So why did he feel like crap? "Sorry," he mumbled. "I wouldn't put it past Levinson."

"I'm not Levinson."

That fact was abundantly clear. He wished Minnie would come back so he could return to safely sulking instead of insulting Thalia's honor. But as there weren't any footsteps on the stairs, he might as well go for broke. "Why do you need me so bad? Actors are a dime a dozen."

It was only after he said it that he realized his words could be taken at least two different ways. He felt his face get hot. Luckily, she looked down at the floor, so she didn't see it.

She almost said something, he realized—but stopped short. Finally, she said, "People are curious about you. They'd pay money to find out what happened to you," in the same cold tone of voice.

And just like that, J.R. was again a commodity to be bought and sold. That unavoidable fact took what interest he had in this woman and buried it six feet under. "I'm not going to take the part, not now, not ever." Part of her face shut down, but not before he caught a glimpse of her disappointment. "And I don't care what Minnie says—you aren't welcome here."

A gasp from behind him didn't do much to break the tension. "J.R.! What did you say?"

This entire situation was spinning out of control, and fast. Her laptop clutched to her chest, Minnie skirted around him and rushed to Thalia saying, "Are you okay?" When Thalia nodded, Minnie fixed him with a glare that could melt glass. "Apologize to our guest, J.R."

Thalia's lower lip quivered—not much, but enough to make him feel like a first-class heel. He should have stuck by his original plan of not talking, but he wasn't backing down.

"I will do no such thing. This is my home, my land and trespassers *will* be shot."

Minnie's eyes narrowed, and suddenly J.R. recalled the time when, more than half-drunk, Hoss had confided that his mother once overpowered him as a teen to keep him from going out with some gang members. Right now, she looked like she was going to take him down and it was going to *hurt*.

"Fine. *Fine.*" He knew he was way overreacting, but he couldn't stop himself. He was the boss around here, for God's sake, and no one seemed to be able to remember that. "She can stay for dinner. I'll leave. But when I get back, she better be gone—for good this time. Do I make myself clear?"

He didn't wait for an answer. He grabbed his coat and hat and made damn sure to slam the door behind him.

He'd almost kissed her.

What a mess.

Five

"I should go." That was the only thing Thalia could do. She'd gambled on coming back here and lost big-time. Any hope she had of signing James Robert Bradley was gone for good now. She'd slapped him, for crying out loud. That wasn't exactly a proven negotiating tactic.

Minnie and Hoss shared a look before Minnie said, "Now, don't you worry about J.R. He's just throwing a little...temper tantrum."

Thalia had seen plenty of big egos throw plenty of fits, but those were usually over petty things like trailer size or catering. This "temper tantrum" was much more intense. Much more personal.

"We're used to it," Hoss added, peeking into the oven. The smells of homemade food filled the room, making another argument for why Thalia should at least stay for dinner.

"Really?" She perched on the edge of the stool, not sure if she could relax enough to actually sit on it. "Does he do this often?" He didn't seem like the kind who had hissy fits.

"Oh, my." Minnie chuckled, and Thalia felt some of the tension leave her shoulders. "When we first moved out here, he was so melodramatic." She sighed, brushing her brow in a fake faint. "Every time someone in town called him out, he'd sulk for days."

"Can't tell you how many fights he got into," Hoss added. "Got to the point where Denny wouldn't let him in the bar for a while." He chuckled. "You can take the diva out of Hollywood, but you can't take Hollywood out of the diva."

Thalia mulled over that information as Minnie set plates around the island. "Does that happen a lot—those tantrums?"

"It's been a couple of years since he threw a good one." Hoss looked like he was going to say something else, but Minnie cleared her throat.

"Thalia, be a dear and get the salt and pepper. When it's just us, we eat at the island."

She knew the compliment was partially misdirection, but she was flattered nonetheless. At least someone in this house liked her. Too bad it wasn't the man she was here for. She wondered what had happened a couple of years ago that had provoked his last fit, but Minnie and Hoss were exchanging meaningful glances again, and she knew that she wasn't going to find out.

Still, they seemed to be in a chatty mood. Maybe they were trying to overcompensate for J.R. She decided to skip the tantrums and start at the beginning. "So you met him on the set of *Hell for Leather?*"

Hoss snorted as he dug out a huge helping of spicy chicken casserole. "Not so much *on* the set. I found him in a bar one night, a few towns over. He had on this huge hat, glasses and a fake mustache. Sitting in the corner, drinking a beer like he didn't know how." Hoss chuckled again. "Trying hard to be invisible and doing a damn lousy job at it."

Something about that statement struck Thalia. A wave of guilt washed over her. J.R. was right. She'd been trying to mount a side attack, using Minnie as cover—because she was desperate. She hadn't considered why he was so adamantly opposed to her offer. Perhaps she'd been in Hollywood for so long that she'd forgotten that people did things for reasons that had nothing to do with money or fame.

"Now, don't you fret," Minnie said, patting her arm. "He'll calm down. You know, he skipped his teenaged years. He was already famous, and his mother…she didn't allow for much deviation." The way the older woman said "mother" reminded Thalia that many people believed that J.R. had had something to do with his mother's unexpected death at forty-two, which was why he'd disappeared so quickly after the funeral. "So when he got out here, he—what's the word?"

"Regressed. Had to look that one up," Hoss said with his mouth full.

"Yes, he regressed. We had our hands full for a few years." She smiled at the memory. "But he settled. He'll settle again."

"What I don't understand is, why is he here? I mean, no one knows where he is. He just disappeared."

"I told you—invisible." Hoss made a swirling circle with his hand and added, "Poof!" for emphasis.

"I think the bigger question is why you're here." Minnie had Thalia locked under the same no-nonsense gaze that she'd been giving J.R. "As much as I enjoy talking about the gowns, I know you're not here for me. Why are you pursuing him?"

Thalia swallowed carefully, afraid that she might choke on her chicken. "It'd be good PR for the movie," she said, almost reflexively. "People want to know what happened to him."

Minnie smiled, but Thalia could tell she wasn't off the hook. Suddenly, she didn't feel as comfortable anymore. But what could she do? Minnie had stuck up for her on multiple occasions and kept her from turning into a Popsicle. At the least, she owed the older woman the truth.

Thalia felt unexpected tears crowding at the corner of her eyes. "If I don't sign him, I don't have a job. Levinson will fire me, and he'll make sure no one else will hire me." She left out the part about her past affair with Levinson, and especially the part about how his wife had destroyed her acting career because of that affair. One humiliation at a time was all she could handle right now while maintaining her composure.

"I see." An uncomfortable silence settled over the table. Thalia was miserable. The worst of it was, she liked Minnie and Hoss, and now she'd used the sincere friendship they'd offered her as a wedge between them and J.R.

No, that wasn't the worst of it. The worst of it was that she had let her feelings get in the way. If she hadn't let her decade-old crush on James Robert Bradley color her motivations, then she could have done a better job negotiating as a professional, not a love-struck teenybopper. She'd tried so hard to justify touching J.R. the first time as something she'd done only because she'd been half-asleep.

This afternoon had showed her how wrong she was. The moment he'd grabbed her, she should have pulled away. The moment he'd looked down into her eyes, she should have thrown up some sort of wall. The moment he'd looked like he'd wanted to kiss her as much as she wanted him to, she should have done…something. Anything that wouldn't have left her wide open to his insults.

"He won't do it, will he?"

Hoss was the one who answered. "I doubt it."

"He doesn't want the notoriety, and he doesn't need the money," Minnie added.

"What *does* he want?" It was some kind of pathetic to have to ask, but she was running out of ideas.

"Well…" Before Hoss could expound on that thought, he grunted. "Oof!" Thalia suspected that Minnie had kicked him.

Right. There was that whole sex thing. He had wanted to kiss her, after all. She could track him down, throw herself at him and seduce him until he was willing to agree to anything, like he'd accused her of doing. Some people operated like that.

The problem was, she knew, deep down, that J.R. wasn't one of those people. And neither was she.

"I don't know if even J.R. knows the answer to that question." It was nice of Minnie to dance around the obvious, but it didn't change things.

Thalia had hit a big, J.R.-shaped brick wall. Clearly, attempting this on his turf was a nonstarter. He'd dug in his heels, big-time. But it wasn't like she could get him to Hollywood, or some other neutral territory, to start over. Hell, she doubted she could do that even to apologize.

The moment the thought crossed her mind, she latched on. She needed to apologize. That might not buy her much goodwill, but it was obvious that there could be no professional discussions while he felt himself the wronged party.

The more this idea bounced around her head, the better she liked it. He'd gone somewhere, after all—somewhere that wasn't his home. Somewhere neutral—or more neutral than here, anyway.

She needed to head toward Beaverhead. It was a small town, to be sure, but she remembered seeing the blinking Budweiser sign in a window. She'd be willing to bet that J. R. Bradley's truck would be parked out front right about now.

She thanked Minnie and Hoss for dinner. Minnie repeated that she was welcome to stop by anytime she was in the neighborhood, but no one made any final-sounding goodbyes.

This wasn't over yet. Not by a long shot.

Denny's was hopping for the middle of the week. Not that J.R. was talking with anyone in the crowd, but as he sat in his usual spot at the end of the bar, he kept an ear open. Maybe it was the weather. The lack of snow made it easy to get out. Whatever it was, it was crowded. The noise of drunken two-stepping, bragging and pool games tried hard to distract J.R. from his little pity party.

Man, he was in so much trouble. Minnie was going to skin him alive—that was, if she didn't kill him outright. He rubbed his face, wondering when things had gone so wrong. He was mad at himself on top of things. He'd been out here for eleven years. He thought he'd gotten real good at dealing with the shadows of his past, but all it took was one woman— one single, beautiful woman—to blow up his world again. Why did he let her get to him?

And why, for the love of all things holy, was he still thinking about her?

As he nursed his third beer, J.R. felt the blast of cold air as the door opened and closed again. That wasn't so unusual. What was different this time was the way the rowdy crowd quieted down for a beat too long, as if they were all collectively staring at the new arrival. J.R. felt the hairs on the back of his neck stand up in a way that had nothing to do with the drop in temperature.

Damn it.

The bar was quiet enough that he heard the clack of Thalia Thorne's boots making straight for him. She slid onto the bar stool next to him, but she didn't say anything until Denny came down. "What'll it be?"

"I'll take a Natural Light," she said, as if that were an everyday thing.

J.R. snorted. "You drink beer?" And not just any beer. Natty Light. That was pretty low-brow for a woman like her.

"I used to," she admitted without looking at him. "When I was in college at OSU, I drank a lot of beer."

"But not in L.A." OSU—he struggled to think which *O* that was. Oklahoma? Yeah, she'd said something about her mom in Oklahoma.

"Not my scene." When Denny slid her the bottle, she thanked him and took a pull.

They sat there. J.R. didn't know what to do. Every time he'd tried to talk to this woman, some sort of social disaster had occurred. On the bright side, Minnie wasn't here to get all offended at his loutish behavior.

He could talk to this woman without losing his temper. He could try, anyway. "How much longer are you gonna keep following me?"

"Beg pardon?" She choked on her swig, and J.R. realized he was going to have to work on his timing.

"You show up at my house despite posted trespassing signs and my explicit wishes. When I finally leave, you barge into my favorite bar." He was proud that he managed to keep his voice level. "What's next, huh?" He almost added, you gonna follow me into the shower? He was stopped by the image that sprang up in his head of her, wet and naked in his bathroom, water streaming down her back, between her breasts—maybe he'd had too much beer. He cleared his throat and tried to shift on his seat without giving anything away.

She didn't say anything for a second, which again struck him as odd. Aside from her inability to respect his wishes to be left alone, she didn't negotiate like anyone else he'd ever known. Hell, even Hoss would have barged into the gap, pressing his case with a nearly religious fervor. Not her. It was almost as if she were here against her will.

Either that, or she was thinking about showers, too.

Crap. He either needed more beer or less beer. And since less was hard to pull off, he said, "Denny, one more."

The old man set the bottle down in front of J.R. "That's your fourth one, bud. You know the rule."

"The rule?" Of course Thalia would barge into *that* gap.

Denny gave her something that might have been a smile on someone less crusty. "I cut him off at four."

"Why?" She was leaning forward, as if Denny were spilling deep, personal secrets instead of company policy.

"Because," J.R. answered for the older man. "More than four and I usually wind up punching someone."

"Or something," Denny added, lifting up the corner of a poster that covered a fist-sized hole in the wall.

"Aw, man, I paid you to get that fixed." And he hadn't been allowed back in the bar for six months. "That was five years ago."

"You paid me, all right." Chuckling, Denny moved back down the counter, leaving J.R. staring at his fourth beer. As much as he wanted to drain the sucker dry, he wasn't ready to go home to face the Minnie-music, so he had to nurse it.

He waited for Thalia to make some sort of comment on his propensity for bar-based violence, but she didn't. Suddenly, J.R. got nervous. What did she know? More specifically, what had Hoss told her?

As if she was reading his mind, she said, "Hoss said he found you in a bar, trying to be invisible."

Damn. She finally looked at him, pivoting her stool around so he got the full view of her sweater-clad chest again. "You don't look so invisible now."

"I don't have to hide anymore." Which was a bold-faced lie, and they both knew it. It was so bold-faced that he heard himself lie some more. "I'm not hiding from you."

"That's why I'm here." She looked at her bottle, her fingernails peeling the label. "I wanted to apologize."

J.R. shot a look around the bar, trying to figure out if the volume had distorted her words. "You wanna *what?*"

"Apologize." She still didn't meet his eyes, but her fingers were doing interesting things with her beer bottle.

Nope, he'd heard her right the first time. "For trespassing?"

When she shook her head, her hair caught the dim light of the bar. For a second, she glowed. Why did she have to be so pretty? He managed not to say that. Score one for his big, fat mouth.

"No." She swung away from him, back to the bar. He

turned his gaze forward, too. Even though they were still sitting next to each other, it put a wall between them. He wasn't
sure if he liked that illusion of distance or not. It was good
because it gave him a little thinking room, but all the same,
he liked looking at her.

Someone on the other side of the bar catcalled, which set
his teeth on edge. Other idiots in this bar apparently liked
looking at her, too.

She didn't seem to notice. "I'm sorry that I didn't realize what I was asking you to do. What I was asking you to
give up."

J.R. forgot all about the catcall, the four-beer limit and
how Minnie was going to kill him. He forgot everything but
the woman sitting next to him. "What?" Deep inside, past
the buzz he was working on, something in him hummed in
recognition—the same pull he'd felt when they'd had dinner together.

She drained the last of her beer—for courage, he wondered? "I should have realized that the thing that made you—"

Whatever she was going to say—and man, did he want to
hear it—was cut off by the huge arm dividing the space between them. The hand slammed into the bar top as a voice
said, "Well, well, lookit what the big star drug in!"

Just when things had started to look up. J.R. didn't have
to see who the voice belonged to. He recognized Jeff "Big
Dog" Dorsey. *As if this evening couldn't get any worse,* he
thought. He hired Dorsey on in the summer to work cattle.
The man was a damn fine cowboy, but a slimy excuse for a
man. "Back off, Dog."

"I ain't talkin' to you, *Hollywood.* I'm talkin' to the purty
lady." He leered down into Thalia's face. "Hi, purty lady."
Thalia shrank back in confusion and not a little bit of fear.

J.R. grabbed Dog's arm and shoved. "I said *back off.*
You're drunk."

"Oooh, I'm scared. Shaking."

"You should be scared." When J.R. stood, fists already clenched, his stool tipped over. In the time before it hit the ground, Dorsey grabbed Thalia's arm. She shot J.R. a look of stark panic.

The next thing J.R. knew, he had Dorsey by the throat and the two of them were flying backward, crashing through tables and chairs until they hit a wall. "You touch her again," he growled, not sure where the threat was going. Instead, he leaned his forearm against Dorsey's windpipe a little harder. The big man's eyes bulged. Good. Everyone would know how dead serious J.R. was.

Dorsey took an off balance swing at J.R.'s midsection, knocking most of the wind out of him. But the blow wasn't enough to push J.R. off entirely.

The rest of the crowd was mostly yelling for Dorsey to knock J.R. to the ground, although in the background, he could hear Denny bellowing for everyone to knock it off or he was gonna call Stan, the local law. J.R. held firm, using his thigh to block Dorsey's last-ditch attempt to rack him.

As Dorsey's eyes started to roll back in his head, J.R. realized he'd lost track of Thalia. He let go of Dorsey and stepped back. The big man dropped to his knees with a *whump,* coughing hard. The crowd quieted as J.R. spun to look at them. Yeah, everyone was at least half-drunk, and yeah, it was a little scuffle, but everyone in here had been rooting for him to take a good punch or three.

He used to like this bar.

Finally, he saw Thalia at the back, cutting her way through the silent crowd. The good news was that she didn't look scared anymore. The bad news was that she seemed a little pissed.

"You like to strangle me!" Dorsey'd gotten most of his voice back. Too bad.

"You treat a woman like that again, and I'll see to it that you never find work around these parts again."

The crowd murmured, half in approval and half in disagreement. J.R. didn't care. He recognized ten or so faces from his summer crew. They knew he fed them well and paid them better. A summer spot at the Bar B Ranch left a man enough to live on for the long winter. Most of the eyes he met nodded in silent agreement. No one wanted to risk their spot.

The crowd parted as he headed back to where Thalia was, her hands on her hips. "Come on," he said, shooting a look back to Denny. The old man shook his head in disappointment. "Let me know if I owe you anything for the chairs."

Denny waved him off.

Thalia grabbed her purse and coat and went outside with him. "What was that?" she demanded once the door of the bar was shut.

"That was me defending you?" Her sudden burst of anger caught him off guard.

"Okay, yes, and I appreciate being defended. But—" she jammed her arms in her coat and then crossed them, giving him a highly critical once-over. He was getting mighty tired of people looking at him like that "—that's how you handle hecklers? No wonder you're busy *not* hiding out here."

When had he become the bad guy here? "Why are you mad at me? Dorsey's the one being a jackass. I was putting him in his place. It's not a big deal."

"It could be, J.R. Maybe not in a bar in the middle of nowhere, but what happens when you pull that crap in the real world? What happens when someone with a camera finds you? You can't beat down just anyone. As it is, you're lucky you're not being sued for assault—and how do you think that would look on a tabloid headline? Because gossip has a life of its own, you know."

No doubt about it—he was the bad guy here. And he still didn't understand what her problem was. Why should she care about what he did? "What is your deal? This place *is* my real world, and things were fine before you showed up. You're the one who turned everyone's head." His words spilled out of him faster than he could figure out what he was going to say. "If you didn't stand out so much, no one would have even noticed me."

Despite the heavy coat—a different one than she'd had on last time—he saw her visibly bristle. "I will not apologize for existing."

"Yeah? Well, you were going to apologize for something, so don't act like it's beneath you."

She threw her hands up and all but snarled at him. "I do not have time for temper tantrums, not all the way out here. If I want ego trips and sexism, I'll go back to Hollywood. There, at least, I can see it coming a mile off." She turned toward her little rental car. "And," she said, spinning on her heel, "I was going to apologize, but it's clear you don't need one and I'm not about to throw a punch to make my point."

"Oh, so it's not okay for me to keep a drunk from manhandling you, but it's fine for you to slap me? Typical," he muttered at her retreating back.

She didn't retreat for long. "Excuse me?" The next thing he knew, she was bearing down on him, and the look in her eye said that punching him was still on the table. "You're allowed to defend my honor from a drunk? You—who asked me if I was Levinson's whore?" She put her hand flat on his chest and shoved. She packed a little more wallop than he would have given her credit for—he had to take a step back to keep his balance.

He grabbed her hand, but didn't pull it away from his chest. Maybe those beers had hit him harder than he thought, because he was having trouble keeping up with her. She was mad at him, that he got. But what she was mad about seemed to change with every other breath that escaped her parted, reddened lips. "I never said *whore*. Don't put words in my mouth."

"You didn't have to. Your meaning was perfectly clear.

Well, in case it's not blisteringly obvious, I'm no one's whore. Not Levinson's, not yours. I don't sleep with people to get the job done, so if that's what you're holding out for, you can keep on holding."

What the heck was she talking about? He wasn't angling for a roll in the sack—was that what she thought? He knew he should back away, disengage. He didn't. "I'm supposed to believe that, after you all but throw a casting couch at Hoss?"

"That. Was. A. Joke." Her eyes flashed in the dim neon light of the bar signs as she gave him another shove. "Or did you abandon your sense of humor in L.A. along with your life?"

They were close now, so close that he felt the warmth of her breath fan out around his face. He still had her hand pinned to his chest. For some reason, he wanted to smile. This was an argument, no doubt about it—but something about it felt real. Honest. Thalia was furious, true, but it felt good to have things out in the open. No pussyfooting around what she wanted, or who he used to be. Their differences were front and center.

"Why are you mad at me?" If they were being honest, then he was going to have to own up to his cluelessness.

"Because you don't seem to understand how your actions—grabbing a woman and questioning her reputation, brawling in a bar—can get away from you. If you did either of those things in my world, J.R., you'd wind up on the evening news, and if you think I'm a pain in your—" she paused and swallowed. She was doing that thing again, where she blushed without seeming to acknowledge her embarrassment "—neck, then you can't imagine how hard the paparazzi will make your life, your family's life."

"You being here makes it hard on me."

Everything about her changed in the space of two heartbeats. The fire in her eyes simmered down to a warm glow. Anytime she wanted to stop looking sweet and beautiful would be great. "I know. That's what I was going to apologize for." Her voice was soft, inviting.

The space between them thinned, and he briefly thought she might be the one to start the kissing. She wanted to—he thought. Then the door of the bar opened, and noise—and a few bodies—poured out.

When she stepped away, he had no choice but to let her go.

Without another word, she turned back to her car. "Hey." He jogged after her—as much as one jogged in boots, anyway. "You're still staying at Lloyd's, right?" Being the smallest of towns, every resident of Beaverhead probably knew the sexy out-of-towner was holed up at Lloyd's. Including Dorsey.

She paused, her hand on the door handle. "J.R., I…" Her voice trailed off, taking whatever she was going to say with it. Then, she got in and drove off.

Six

The truck—J.R.'s truck—was still out there. It was dark, so Thalia wasn't one hundred percent sure that it was actually him, but something told her he'd followed her back to Lloyd's.

What the heck was she supposed to do about this? J.R. had all but accused her of stalking him—somewhat rightly—and now he was staking her out? Was this normal?

No, there was nothing normal about anything this evening. Not the part where she slapped him, not the part where he nearly strangled a guy for touching her and not the moment of blistering honesty in the parking lot. Not a normal event in the bunch.

So the better question was: Was this dangerous? She'd pushed J.R. further than she'd meant to, and every one of her attempts to negotiate with him backfired on her in one way or another. Despite how much she irritated J.R.—which she knew was a lot—and despite how much he was driving her bonkers—an almost equal amount—she didn't think he was a physical threat to her.

* * *

She wasn't going to be able to sleep, much less take a hot shower, knowing he was out there without knowing why. And she was not about to go back outside and ask him.

When her cell rang, she jumped so hard she almost tore down the drapery she was hiding behind. She didn't recognize the number, but she thought it was a Montana area code. "Hello?"

"Thalia? This is Minnie Red Horse. Have you seen J.R.?"

Thalia let out a rush of air. "Yes. I went to apologize at the local bar."

After a momentary pause, Minnie said, "Oh. Do you have any idea when he'll be home? He's not answering his phone, and Denny says he left with you."

Thalia winced. They'd left at the same time, which was entirely different than leaving together. "He's not with me now, but I could try calling him for you." That way she could figure out if he was the one watching her window or not.

"Thank you, dear." Minnie gave her the number and they hung up.

Thalia looked at her phone. This wasn't about the part or the movie anymore. This felt like the point of no return. She could go one way or the other. She could call him, or she could ignore the truck outside.

She dialed. She couldn't see any movement in the truck, but then he picked up. "Hello?"

"Are you following me?"

In response, the overhead light in the truck flipped on, and she saw J.R. in profile. "I'm not so much following you as keeping an eye on you." He cleared his throat. "Are you up there?"

She turned on the small bedside lamp. It wasn't a lot of light, but it was enough that he could at least see her in profile. Luckily, the flannel pajamas she'd bought at J.C. Penney didn't lend themselves to being see-through. "Is there a difference between following me and keeping an eye on me? Because if there is, I'm not seeing it."

"Everyone in town probably knows where you're at, and Dog isn't the kind of man to let something go—not until he's sobered up." He paused, and she wished she could see his eyes. "I'm making sure he doesn't come back to prove his point."

"Oh." That was a pretty good reason. She might have conflicting feelings about J.R., but she definitely didn't want to see that brute again. Ever.

That begged another question. "Why do you care? I mean, I've been nothing but trouble for you. You could hang me out to dry."

He snorted. "I see nothing's changed about Hollywood."

"What's that supposed to mean?"

"Just because you trespass on *my* property and flirt with *my* best friend and attract all the wrong kinds of attention at *my* bar doesn't mean I'd stand by and let anything happen to you. A real man makes sure a lady is safe."

Part of Thalia melted. Maybe it was because she'd been hung out to dry on more than one occasion. After all, Levinson had let her take all of the fall for their failed affair, and she'd once fancied that he loved her. As incredible as it seemed now, she'd once fancied that she'd loved him. Just another example of letting her emotions get in the way of business.

This was different. Knowing—and believing—that J.R. would defend her instead of throwing her to the wolves was a gift in and of itself. That he thought of her as a lady, despite how wrong things had gone? *Melt.*

But as one part of her melted, another part of her wanted to throw things at him. "What is it with you? Okay, so I wasn't invited the first time. It's not like I cut a lock and snuck into your house. Minnie invited me back the second time. And I'm not flirting with Hoss. He's a nice man and all, but I'm not interested in him. Ugh. It would be like kissing my brother. And I can't help it if this town is populated with Neanderthals."

She expected him to come back with the myriad of ways this whole thing was all her fault, but he didn't say anything. The silence stretched between them, and she found herself wondering if he was done talking or what.

"That happen a lot?" was what he finally said, startling her.

"Which part?"

"Getting hung out to dry? Or what is it they say now? Thrown in front of the bus?"

"Thrown under the bus." She smiled at him, not that he could see it. Who would have guessed that the man who was once the physical embodiment of cool couldn't even handle a catchphrase?

"Yeah. That. The Hollywood I used to know was every man—and woman—for themselves. That ever happen to you?"

She exhaled, fogging up the window. Levinson had not only thrown her under the bus, but he'd backed it up over her a few times for good measure. She didn't want to tell J.R. that. He had obviously already formed an opinion of her. He hated Levinson, and with good reason. If she told J.R. how Levinson had all but tied her to the bumper of the bus, it would destroy what little respect he had for her. "It's Hollywood. Nothing I can't handle." She heard J.R. chuckle. "What?"

"I'm going to take that as a *yes*. How long you been there?"

She didn't like this, not one bit. Despite the physical distance between them, it felt like he was not only digging into her past, but getting close to striking pay dirt. It made her nervous, like she was giving something up.

How long had it been since someone had asked her these basic questions? A long time. After the affair with Levinson had blown up in her face, she'd retreated into herself. People—men—didn't ask where she was from. Was that because they were a self-absorbed lot? Or because she never gave anyone the chance to get past that first wall?

"Must be doing some hard thinking up there," J.R. mused into the silence. "Or did you forget? Hollywood can do that, you know."

"I've been there ten years. I haven't forgotten."

"Ah, now. And you can't be much over…" She could only wonder what age he was going to say. "Well, I guess you went out when you were a teenager."

She could picture the grin on his face—small, hidden beneath the beard—but at heart, the same grin that he'd had on in all those posters she'd taped up in her room when she was a teenager. Somehow, back when she'd envisioned meeting James Robert Bradley, this particular scenario never played out in her head—him making guesses on how old she was.

He'd probably keep dancing around it until she told him. This was one of the few plusses of not being an actress. Her age wasn't an immediate disqualifier. "I turned thirty in September, if that's what you wanted to know."

"Hmm." The sound he made—closer to a purr than a thoughtful observation—sent little sparks of electricity racing up and down the skin on the back of her hand. "That's not old."

She wouldn't let that count as flattery. "Boy, you have been gone a long time. I'm all but a dinosaur these days."

"Wonder what that makes me? No, don't answer that."

Not that she was going to, because then she'd have to tell him that he was clearly one of those men who only got better with age, like Cary Grant or Gregory Peck. And then she'd get all swoony again, and every time she did that, she managed to stick her foot in her mouth. "It's different," he went on, missing her awkward silence. "You've only been there for ten years. I was there for…twenty-one years."

"Really?" It seemed like a long time—but also not quite long enough. "I always kind of thought you were born there."

"Nope. St. Louis. My mother had me doing commercials when I was a baby." His voice seemed to grow softer. She couldn't tell if he was holding the phone away from his mouth or getting all sentimental. "We moved to Hollywood when I was four."

"You were so young."

"Oh, yeah." He exhaled into the phone. "You know what I wanted to be when I grew up?"

"No." She didn't know where he was going with this trip down memory lane. If she had to describe this current exchange, she'd have to call it chitchat, the conversation of two friends. It bordered on sharing, and she was afraid she didn't want the conversation to end.

"A firefighter, an astronaut and a cowboy. Oh, and an army man." He paused, and when he spoke again, she could hear the nostalgia in his voice. "I went back to St. Louis once, after I came out here. Didn't recognize anything. Not even the house I grew up in." He cleared his throat. "That was a long time ago."

"You didn't want to be an actor?"

"It's what my mother wanted."

"You were good at it." Obviously. They didn't usually give Oscars out of pity.

"It was never my choice, Thalia."

The weight of those words tried to cave in her chest. Gone was the nostalgic tone, the sentimental-sounding sighs. Heck, he didn't even sound like he'd been drinking. He was dead serious.

She felt so, so guilty, an emotion that she'd gotten used to pretending she didn't experience. She'd asked him to take the part, and he'd said no. Instead of respecting that choice, she had kept coming at him. And what made it worse was that he'd been right about the bar fight. He hadn't been sued for loutish behavior yet. He was, relatively speaking, safe out here. She was the one who could expose him. If people came looking for him, it would be because of her. If he went viral, it would all trace back to the day she landed in Montana.

But to show guilt was to show weakness, and no matter how personal this conversation seemed, she wouldn't grovel. So she tried to deflect. "A cowboy, huh?"

"Yup."

He didn't come up with another wild tangent. For the life of her, she couldn't read his mind. The silence started to bug her. Maybe she couldn't bring herself to apologize for not honoring his choice, but she still owed him something. "I'm sorry I slapped you earlier. You were right, that was uncalled for."

"It's okay. I crossed a line I shouldn't have. My apologies for that. It's just…"

When his voice trailed off, Thalia found herself leaning into the window, hoping to hear what he had to say. A story below her, she saw J.R. shift in his seat, leaning forward until he was looking up at her. She couldn't see his eyes, darn it, but she still felt a connection with him as clearly as if she was sitting across the table from him.

"Minnie's probably worried about me." He leaned back, his whole face disappearing into the cab of his truck.

"Yeah." Right—she was supposed to tell him that exact thing. "You should probably get home."

The dome light flipped off, and she thought he'd hung up on her. Then she heard him say, "I won't let anyone bother you, Thalia."

She pressed her hand to the window again, wishing she could touch him, wishing she could feel his strong hand cover hers again. "I know, J.R."

The call ended. Thalia turned out the light, but she stood at the window for a few more moments, knowing he would keep her safe.

The odd thing was, she wanted to do the same for him— to protect him. To make sure that he didn't wind up as fodder for the paparazzi.

This was all backward. There was no such thing as bad PR, after all. J.R. making a few headlines would add a big boost to the movie's bottom line.

Standing there in the dark, watching his truck, she knew she couldn't do it. She wasn't the kind of person who let someone destroy themselves for a strong opening weekend.

She wouldn't do that to him.

"I don't like this wind." Hoss tucked his chin into his coat as they headed back to the ranch house after another grueling afternoon of breaking ice. "Nope. Don't like it at all."

"What?" J.R. tried to focus on what Hoss was saying, but it wasn't easy. He was cold—nothing new there. But the cold on top of the bone-deep exhaustion made doing much of anything hard. Hell, a few fields over, he'd lost the grip on his ax midswing and nearly decapitated his best friend.

Hoss snorted. "What time *did* you get home last night?"

J.R. groaned. Hoss already knew the answer—three-thirty. "Late enough."

"Well, I don't like this wind."

J.R. sat up in the saddle, paying a little more attention to the weather. The wind cut down out of the north with bitter speed, but the air felt heavy. "Snow?"

"Snow," Hoss agreed, burrowing deeper into his coat. "Lots of it. And soon."

"How soon?" Mentally, he slapped his head. If he'd been aware of his surroundings, he'd have started moving some cattle into the more sheltered fields. Maybe it wouldn't hit for another day or two. Maybe they'd have time.

"Weather says tomorrow night." Hoss tipped his hat back and sniffed the air. "If we're lucky."

Damn it. "Better check the generators when we get back." The ranch house was well equipped to handle a blizzard. The fireplaces in each room kept the house warmish on their own, but after the first blizzard, J.R. had invested in several superpowered generators for the house and the barn. They had snowshoes, snowmobiles and enough food to last them a month.

He had a ton of books, and Minnie was fond of Scrabble. Plus, they needed the snow to hedge their bets against a dry summer. In all reality, snow was not a bad thing.

That didn't mean J.R. had to like it.

He liked it a whole lot less when he and Hoss crested the last hill and saw Thalia's rental car in front of his house again. "Oh, no."

"What is she doing out here?" Hoss asked. The fact that Hoss hadn't grabbed this opportunity to tease J.R. showed how worried his best friend was about the weather. "Don't she know it's going to snow?"

"City folk," J.R. grumbled, pushing his horse on as much as he dared in this wind.

The weather took a lousy situation and made it downright dangerous. Bad enough that Thalia felt free to drop by any old time she felt like it; worse that her presence had led to him being banned from his favorite bar for the rest of the winter. All of that was inconvenient, annoying.

But to have someone who had been so demonstrably unaware of the weather driving in blizzard conditions—hell, even a regular heavy snow—was a recipe for disaster. People died in this kind of weather. They drove off the road or got hit by a plow. Or they got disorientated and froze to death a few feet from their house.

A golden, sunshine woman like Thalia wouldn't stand a chance against a Montana blizzard. He didn't have a doubt in his mind about that. And he knew, even though she drove him well past the point of distraction, that he'd do whatever he could to keep her safe.

He didn't know what that *whatever* would mean.

He and Hoss got the horses fed and blanketed before they hurried inside. J.R. couldn't say that he was exactly *happy* to see Thalia, not under the circumstances. When she turned her pretty face to him, and he watched her eyes light up because she was glad to see him, well, damn. He was glad to see her, too.

"Before you say anything," she began without any further ado, "I'm not here about the part."

The effect this statement had on him was unexpected. Maybe he'd gotten a little too cold out in that wind, but a weird, light-headed feeling made his scalp tingle. "Oh?"

"Everything okay?" Hoss stepped around J.R., wrapping one of his arms around Thalia's shoulder and giving her an awkward squeeze. Thalia gave J.R. a look and a half smile, and he heard her voice say, "It would be like kissing my brother." The tingly feeling got a little stronger.

"Yes, it's fine." Thalia straightened, and Hoss's arm fell away. "I came to say goodbye."

Minnie made a noise, and for the first time, J.R. noticed her. She looked like she'd been crying, or something close to it—watery eyes, red nose she kept wiping with a tissue. Thalia turned and patted Minnie on the arm, like she was trying to comfort her.

What the heck was going on?

"You sure about that?" Hoss was looking worried now, too, which only made the feeling that J.R. was missing something important get even stronger.

"It'll be okay." Thalia smiled at Hoss, but J.R. could see that it didn't reach her eyes. She was lying—about what?

"Anytime you're out this way, you stop by," Minnie said with a hug. "It's been a pleasure having you out here." Then she patted Thalia's cheek. "I know it's hard to see now, but it'll work out. I believe that."

The way Minnie—and Hoss—were talking was almost like they were trying to get Thalia to stay. And here J.R. had been trying to get rid of her for days.

He didn't know what was going on, but he wasn't entirely

sure he wanted her to leave. Only because of the weather, he quickly told himself.

Thalia's smile was more real this time. "I know. If I get any extra seats to an awards show, I'll call you and you can see all those dresses in person."

Instead of acting like a kid on Christmas morning, like J.R. would have expected, Minnie sniffled again. "That'd be wonderful, dear, but call your mother first."

"Yeah, don't let the turkeys get you down," Hoss added, throwing his arm around her shoulder again. "You'll call me if you find a good casting couch, right?"

"If something comes up, you're at the top of my list."

Then Hoss and Minnie stepped back, and it was just Thalia and J.R. "So you're going back to California."

"Yes." She was lying again. He could tell by the way her eyes didn't move. She took a step toward him, her hand extended. "J.R., it has been a true pleasure meeting you."

Something about this goodbye felt so final. He didn't like it, and he didn't like that he didn't like it. He'd wanted her to go. He'd told her so in no uncertain terms. And yet... "Likewise." He took her hand in his and held it. The heat that coursed through her warmed him down to his toes. This was less erotic than when she'd touched his face, but no less dizzying. He would have sworn the room was spinning.

Don't go, he almost said. Before he could force the words out, she pulled her hand back and said, "And you don't have to worry. I won't tell Levinson where you are."

"You won't?" It was like he understood each individual word, but strung together, they didn't make any sense.

"No." She lowered her eyes, but looked at him through her thick lashes. "I won't let anyone bother you."

The room—hell, the world—spun even faster, so much so that J.R. had to put his hand on the countertop to steady himself. No one—other than Minnie and Hoss—had ever promised to protect him. And neither of them ever looked at J.R. like Thalia did.

Then she grinned and the tension broke. "Of course, I'm not your agent, so…"

"Yeah." J.R. had to clear his throat. "I'm gonna fire that man."

"Be sure to sign him to a nondisclosure agreement first. That way, if he ever tells anyone else, you can sue him."

"Oh, okay." Actually, that was a good idea. Why hadn't he thought of that before? Probably because he'd never done anything with contracts beyond sign them. His mother had always negotiated everything. J.R. had never figured out if she'd gotten what she'd wanted.

They stood there for a moment. She needed to leave—the weather wasn't going to wait on her—but he couldn't quite bring himself to be the one to say goodbye first.

"Thalia—" he began, but the shrill siren of the emergency weather radio cut him off. Everyone jumped at the sound.

Seconds later, the nasal voice of the weather guy came on. "The following is from the National Weather Service. The following counties are under a blizzard warning as of 4:00 p.m.…"

"Is that here?" Thalia looked at the clock on the stove. Three-fifteen. "I should go. I'm supposed to catch a flight out of Billings tonight."

"You won't make it." That seemed like a simple fact, but the look Thalia shot him made it clear that she took it as a personal attack on her driving skills.

"I'm perfectly capable—" This time, she was cut off by the phone ringing.

Minnie answered it while Thalia glared at him. Maybe he should get her to sign one of those nondisclosure things—just in case.

"Yes, she's here. Yes, we heard." Minnie's forehead was so knotted up with worry that her brows were in danger of swapping places. "No, that's okay. You go on. We'll take care of her." She hung up and looked at J.R. "That was Lloyd. He wants to go stay with his daughter—she's got a generator." Her gaze pleaded with J.R. He could almost hear her saying, *Don't put that woman out in this weather. She won't make it.* "He said he'd leave the key in the mailbox if we needed it."

Minnie was right. In that moment, the path forward became crystal clear. "Thalia, you'll stay here with us."

"I'm leaving. I thought that's what you wanted."

"You will stay." Thalia's mouth opened, no doubt with a snappy comeback at the ready, but when he added, "As my guest," she closed it again, looking a little off balance. How nice that J.R. wasn't the only one who felt like that.

"All of my things are at Lloyd's. I was going to swing by on my way out of town."

Women, J.R. thought. If he were the one leaving town, he'd have that car packed up, first thing. "Minnie's got stuff you can wear."

"No." Thalia's tone was insistent. "I have things I need." He saw her swallow. "Prescriptions I have to take."

Damn.

"I'll go get my things. I'll come right back."

The weather siren went off again. J.R., Hoss and Minnie shared a look. Thalia didn't have two hours. "Fine. Get your coat. I'll drive you."

"You don't have to do that."

"Yes, I do. I have four-wheel drive." Thalia probably only saw off-road vehicles stuck in traffic, but his Jeep could handle anything below two-foot drifts. If he drove real fast, they'd make it fine. He hoped.

"But—"

"No buts. Either I drive or you don't get your things." He turned to go. "I'll bring the Jeep up."

"I'll have a bag ready for you in a second." Minnie was pulling muffins and granola bars out. "Just in case."

"You know where the rope is?" Hoss asked.

"Yeah. You see to the generators." J.R. looked at Thalia, who seemed confused. *City folk,* he thought. "Get your coat. I'll pull up in front."

At least this time, she didn't argue with him—with any of them. J.R. walked through the gale-force wind, grabbed the bundle of nylon rope and fired up the Jeep. He bought a new one every three years—life out here was hard on vehicles.

The moment he pulled around to the front, Thalia and Minnie hurried out the front door. Thalia slid into the passenger seat. Minnie shoved a full bag, no doubt packed with energy foods and bottled water, and a bundle of blankets into the backseat and flat-out ran for the house without another word.

Just in case, Minnie had said.

Just in case they got stuck in a snowdrift.

Seven

Thalia sat in the passenger seat, fuming. First, J.R. couldn't get rid of her fast enough. Now he was all but holding her hostage. Yes, the wind had been vicious—but was it that much worse than it had been the first day she'd driven out here? She didn't think so.

"This is ridiculous," she said after they'd left the gravel road behind. She'd made this trip enough to know that they were only fifteen minutes outside of Beaverhead. At least, they would have been fifteen minutes if she'd been driving. J.R. seemed to be going *fast*. "I could have done this myself. You didn't need to drive me."

He had the nerve to sit there and snort in what sounded like derision.

"I can take care of myself, you know," she shot out at him.

"Thalia, the sooner you figure out this isn't Hollywood, the better off we'll all be."

The phrase *you're not the boss of me* was on the tip of her tongue, but even she knew how immature that would sound. "I'm fully aware I'm not in California."

"Ever have a blizzard down in Oklahoma?"

"It snowed sometimes, sure." A rare enough event, but she had wonderful memories sledding out at her grandfather's farm and throwing snowballs at her mom.

"I didn't say snow. I said blizzard."

As if to punctuate his point, one, then two, then two million snowflakes suddenly appeared. One minute, the road was right there. The next, she couldn't see the center stripe, much less the pavement. Each snowflake seemed to slam into the windshield with true menace.

"Uh—wow." Snow had always been a happy, joyful thing when she was a kid—no school, lots of cocoa and cookies, fluffy snow angels.

This was another beast entirely.

She felt foolish all over again, just as she had a few days ago, when she'd stood on his porch in a dress and tights and nearly froze to death. She'd grossly misjudged the situation, and now she felt stupid for having protested as much as she had.

Another emotion tempered that feeling—gratitude. J.R. had a white-knuckle grip on the steering wheel, but as far as she could tell, he hadn't slowed down. He'd known this was coming—and had refused to let her drive off into it. Just like he'd refused to let that hick get close to her.

"Timing is everything." His voice had dropped back into the no-nonsense tone he'd used to inform her he was driving. "I'll get you close to the door. Did you see where the mailbox was?"

"Yes. Lloyd showed me, in case I was out late." The whole thing had seemed hopelessly old-fashioned at the time. She was used to hotels with doormen and key cards. But now? Old-fashioned ruled.

"We'll do this together, but we've got to be fast."

The next thing she knew, he was skidding to a stop, and Lloyd's house popped out from behind a curtain of white. He reached into the back, and when he sat back up, he had a huge bundle of rope in his hands. Silently, he leaned over her and tied the rope to the door handle. "You get out first, but I'll be right behind you. We'll do this together," he repeated. "You've got to stay with me, okay?"

"Okay." She didn't know what was scaring her more—the snow or how serious he was about it.

He touched his gloved hand to hers and gave her a crooked smile, then he opened her door and all but shoved her out.

The wind. Oh, lord, the wind. What had she thought? That this wind wasn't much different from that first day? Maybe, maybe not. This wind wasn't alone. It drove each snowflake into her face with a ruthlessness that took her breath away. Snowflakes? These were more like ice knives, each bent on world domination.

"Move!" J.R. shouted before she was pushed away from the Jeep.

Right. To stand still was to die. J.R. must have driven up onto the front lawn, because she could actually see the front door and the mailbox a few feet away. Fighting the wind with every step, she pushed her way forward until she got a hand on the doorknob.

J.R. was right behind her. As far as she could tell, he had a fistful of her coat in his hand, but she wasn't about to complain. She got the lid of the mailbox open and fished out the key to the front door. The wind almost whipped it right out of her hand, but she got her pinkie finger looped through the keychain and held on.

Finally, after what felt like four false starts, she got the door unlocked and they fell into the house. A few inches of drifted snow came in with them, but Thalia and J.R. got to their feet and got the door shut. The relief she felt was physical, except for the fact they were only halfway. "Two minutes," he said, and she was off.

Thank heavens she'd at least packed her stuff before she'd gone to say goodbye. She grabbed her suitcase—with her birth control pills in it—and the shopping bags with all her winter clothes in seconds. When she flew down the stairs, struggling to hang on to her stuff, J.R. was leaning against the door, looking beat. The door was mostly shut, but she saw he still had a hold of the rope, which was wedged in the door. The wind was pushing at the door so hard, J.R. had to dig in his heels to keep his balance.

His gaze flicked over her with cold-blooded efficiency. "Three bags?"

"Yes." She braced herself for some sort of comment on women and clothes, but he didn't say anything.

With a sigh, he held out his hand. "Give me the two shopping bags so you can hold on to the rope. Whatever you do, don't let go of the rope."

"Okay." She tried to swallow, but her fear was becoming a thing so real she had half a mind to remind it to hang on to the rope, too.

J.R. turned the knob to lock it from the inside, and Thalia set the key on the hall table. If they didn't have to fumble around the mailbox and lock, they'd make it to the truck faster. "Ready?"

She nodded, and he opened the door. The wind jumped at the chance to rush in again, but—maybe for the first time—Thalia was ready for it. Head down, shoulders set, her bag in one hand and the rope in the other, she pushed through it, keeping her eyes locked on J.R.'s back. The only time she looked away was to make sure the door shut behind her. Lloyd had been such a nice host—she'd hate to leave his house full of snow.

By the time she got turned back around, she couldn't see J.R. anymore. A spike of panic stabbed at her throat, making it hard to breathe. She couldn't see anything; she couldn't feel anything but the cold that burrowed under her skin. She couldn't do this. She wasn't sure she even remembered what *this* was.

Then the rope jerked in her hand, pulling her forward so hard she almost stumbled. He was pulling her into safety, she realized, when the rope jerked again. Two more tugs, and the outline of the Jeep came into view. "Still there?" he roared over the wind as he physically hauled her into the vehicle. She realized he must have untied the rope, because, leaning across her body, he threw it outside before pulling the door shut.

The panic was still tight around her throat, smothering her with the realization that if she'd tried to do this by herself, she'd have died. J.R. had saved her from herself. She threw her arms around his neck, any words of thanks she had stuck in the back of her throat with sobs of terror she couldn't voice.

J.R. froze for a second, then his arms wrapped around her, pulling her into his chest. "You're still here," he murmured into her hair before he pressed his lips against her forehead. The touch pushed her panic back and down into her stomach, and she was able to breathe again. "I won't let anything hurt you. But we've got to go."

"Okay," she said as she released him. Not so much because she was all better now, but because they had to keep moving.

Now was probably the time to start praying.

The going was slower this time. Every so often, the winds would relent enough that the stripes on the road would pop up in surprising relief. The snow was something else, but the wind was blowing the road somewhat clear. Every time that happened, J.R. would put the pedal to the metal. Which meant his top speed was probably close to forty miles per hour, then would drop back down into the twenties. It was like bunny hopping in slow motion.

At one point, the wind died back in time to see a post sticking out of the snowbank. J.R. cut the wheel hard to the right.

Clawing for the door handle, Thalia let out a little scream as the truck skidded.

"Easy," J.R. said—the first thing he'd said since they'd left Lloyd's.

Thalia wanted to yell at the man—what about this was easy? And how did driving like a maniac make it any easier? She bit her tongue. He hadn't killed them yet, after all, and she didn't want to distract him and risk hastening their demise.

She was pretty sure they were on the gravel road that led to the ranch, but damned if she could see anything but the snow. However, J.R. seemed to know where he was going. She had no choice but to trust him.

The world had disappeared completely. It felt like the world inside this Jeep was the only thing in existence. Maybe hell wasn't hot, she thought as she tried to see something— anything. Maybe it was unending, white cold.

Suddenly, off to their left, a sputtering burst of firework red broke through the snow. "What the…?"

"Flares," J.R. said, turning the Jeep at a saner rate of speed. He didn't sound shocked about this. "Hang on."

The vehicle jumped and shuddered, as if they were now driving over curbs. Another flare of color cut the white. This time, it was closer, and straight ahead of them. J.R. laid on the horn.

Two more flares cut through the snow, but instead of shooting up into the sky like a Roman candle, they were waving in front of the truck.

"Made it." J.R. may have acted all calm, cool and collected over there, but Thalia heard the sheer relief in his voice.

When the flares got close to the hood, J.R. swung wide and turned the Jeep. The ranch house loomed out from behind the curtain of white like a ghost, hulking and dark. "Damn. Already lost power," J.R. muttered.

That seemed bad, but Thalia remembered him telling Hoss

to get the generators. Maybe the power outage was a temporary thing.

A bundle of fur that looked more like a bear than a man came toward them. "Get your bags," J.R. said, jerking his chin toward the backseat.

Thalia handed her things through the window to Hoss, who disappeared back into the house and then reappeared. "Ready?" J.R. asked seconds before the passenger door was opened.

Without a word, Hoss scooped her up, then turned around. He paused, which didn't make any sense to Thalia—why weren't they running for the house? Then she heard J.R. shout, "Okay!" behind Hoss at the same time she realized Hoss had a rope tied around his waist.

Oh. Duh, Hoss was waiting for J.R. to grab hold. Then their little people train moved into the house. It couldn't have taken more than three minutes, but to Thalia, it felt like hours of being carried through the wilderness. Hoss appeared to be wearing the buffalo robe again, and the snowflakes stuck to the fur. He looked like a yeti.

Soon enough, though, they were being pulled inside the house. Minnie was braced against the door, yanking on the rope hand-over-hand. Hoss managed to set Thalia down on her feet, but J.R. stumbled in and went down on one knee before Minnie could get the door shut behind him.

"Hot damn, now *that's* a blizzard," Hoss announced as he threw off his robe and helped J.R. to his feet. "We were starting to get a little worried about you all."

"You and me both," J.R. muttered as he pulled off his coat. He didn't look exactly steady on his feet. Thalia went to his side and looped her arm around his waist. When he leaned against her, she felt inexplicably good. This wasn't on the same level as him saving her life, but at least she was helping him a little. "Power?"

"Yeah, about that." Hoss looked down at his feet as he

kicked off his snow-covered boots. "The generator won't turn over. If it was lighter, I'd be able to figure out what the deal was, but…" He sounded uncharacteristically defeated.

J.R. sagged against her a little more. "We've got wood, right?"

"Tons."

J.R. squeezed her a little tighter and said, "We'll be fine, then."

Minnie swooped into action, gathering up the coats and shooing everyone back to the kitchen. Thalia wanted to look a little more at the house she was going to be staying in for the foreseeable future—surely there was more to it than a cozy kitchen—but it was all she could do to keep walking. She and J.R. moved slowly, still leaning on each other despite having removed their coats and boots. Maybe it was the cold, or maybe it was the near-death experience that had Thalia still shaking. Whatever it was, she felt warmer and safer tucked under J.R.'s arm than she had in a long time, blizzards notwithstanding.

Minnie plunked them down on a big couch in front of the fire—a couch Thalia was sure hadn't been there a few hours ago. Not that it mattered. The couch was only a few feet from the fire, and the other chairs had been pulled in close to book-end it. It made the otherwise large space feel small and cozy.

She and J.R. slid down onto the leather. Part of her brain realized she was, for lack of a better word, being cuddled by him, and that part tried hard to get swoony.

Another part of her was filled with such an upwelling of gratitude—both to J.R. and to Hoss and Minnie—that she felt a little teary. For as long as she'd been in Hollywood, she'd been on her own, no one to lean on, no one willing to help her handle the constant bumps along the way. The last time anyone had helped her—out of the goodness of their heart and not because they wanted her to be beholden to them—had been… Well, Mom had offered to pay her way home after Thalia had been blacklisted. The thing she'd had to learn the hard way was no one else would be there for her. She was all she had.

Out here, in the proverbial middle of nowhere? J.R. hadn't let her drive off to her doom. Instead, he'd risked his life to make sure she had her things. Minnie was fussing over them with tea and hot soup. And Hoss had taken up residence in one of the chairs and apparently was recounting each and every blizzard they'd weathered out here in great detail. These people had gone out of their way to make sure she was welcome, safe and cared for. At least, they had eventually, in J.R.'s case. And they didn't do it because they wanted a favor for later or because it'd look good on the internet. They did it because that's the way they lived—helping out a neighbor, taking care of a friend.

She'd never known anyone like J.R. And, as she nestled into his arm, she knew she'd never meet another. "Thank you," she whispered so as not to interrupt Hoss's stories.

He didn't respond.

Eight

"Thalia, honey, you must be exhausted." Minnie maneuvered through the furniture to stand in front of her. "Let me show you to your room. Hoss got the fire going while you were gone, so it's fairly warm."

"Oh. Okay." Yes. Seeing other parts of the house was probably preferable to being both snuggled and ignored by J.R. But when she went to stand, J.R.'s arm weighed heavy over her shoulder.

She turned to look at him and saw his head was tucked down on to his chest and his eyes were closed. Ah. That buoyed her spirits—he wasn't ignoring her. He was asleep. Moving slowly, she lifted his arm away and then set his hand in his lap. He didn't even stir.

That was probably her fault, too. She'd turned off her light and gone to bed fairly early—maybe ten o'clock? How long had he sat outside in that truck? Add that to the stress of driving through a blizzard. No wonder the man was exhausted. She was pretty whipped by the whole day, herself.

Minnie had gathered up Thalia's things. Hoss joined them, carrying a huge kettle of water. Thalia took the two shopping bags and they headed up the back stairs. Minnie led the way with a flashlight.

"Is it going to be a problem without power?" Because, honestly, she'd been as close to freezing to death in the last week as she ever wanted to be.

"As long as the fires are burning, you'll be fine," Minnie said at the top of the stairs. Then she turned left down a long hall. "You've got your own bathroom. Can't promise the water will be warm, but at least it'll work. We heat the water for washing on the stove."

So showers were out. "Sounds good." She wasn't about to look the gift of running water in the mouth right now. Instead, she was going to be thankful for being able to wash her face and flush a toilet. It was the little things in life.

Minnie opened the door, and Thalia stepped into exactly the kind of room she'd expected to find. A stone hearth with a blazing fire and a mantle that looked carved from an entire tree took up one wall; wood paneling covered all the others, like downstairs. The big difference was that a huge four-poster bed complete with bed curtains stood in the middle of the room. The bed, while large, looked soft and inviting, the rug appeared to be Navajo, and instead of the animal heads she might have expected, framed art of mountains and trees decorated the place. It beat the heck out of Lloyd's sixties flashback.

"Bathroom's this way," Hoss said, going through a door on the opposite side. "I'll fill the sink for you. It'll be warm for a little bit."

Minnie set the bag down on a cedar chest at the end of the bed. "Let me get those curtains for you. They'll help hold in the heat," she added as she pulled three of the four curtains, but left the side facing the fire open.

Three hours ago, Thalia had been headed home. If she'd

started for Billings instead of coming to say goodbye, she'd probably be in a ditch somewhere, wondering if anyone would find her before she ran out of gas. Now, she was being settled into a guest room half the size of her whole apartment by nice people who were going to feed her and keep her warm. Thalia must have looked a little shell-shocked. God knew she felt it. Minnie came up to her and patted her on the arm in an inherently motherly way. "There's no need to worry, sweetie. We've weathered worse out here. I'm sure the boys will be able to get the generators going tomorrow, and we've got a whole garage of wood out back. We can stay out here for a month, easy."

Thalia's throat closed up on her, pulling down the corners of her mouth and making any sort of polite response all but impossible. A month? Did that mean she would have to spend Valentine's Day with J.R.? And was that a bad thing or a good thing? How was she supposed to get back to Hollywood?

Beyond that, who would miss her? Levinson might, but only because she wasn't at his beck and call. He wouldn't be worried about her, just the work she wasn't able to do. Mom knew she'd come to Montana, but unless this was the kind of blizzard that made the evening news, Mom would assume no news was good news. That was for the best, Thalia decided. She didn't want Mom to be frantic and unable to get a hold of her.

No one else would notice she was gone. She had a few work friends she ate lunch with, that sort of thing, but no roommates, no boyfriends. No close friends. No one who cared about her. She'd been facing another lifeless Valentine's Day with nothing but a solitary card from Mom to mark the occasion.

Everything was different here. She barely knew these people, but J.R. had risked his life to keep her safe, and Minnie and Hoss had welcomed her with open arms. She mattered to them. And more and more, they mattered to her, too. That realization choked her up.

Her lack of words was drowned out by the howling of the wind that seemed to be trying to pull the house apart, piece by piece.

"I've got to check on the pork chops," Minnie said. "Dinner will be in a few."

Thalia managed to nod. Dinner. And after that? She had a nice room—right across the hall from J.R. She was here for the duration. She might as well make the most of it.

J.R. sat as still as he could, straining to hear footsteps over the wind. When he was sure everyone was upstairs, he got up and went to the bathroom. The water from the tap was one step above ice cubes, but he splashed it on his face anyway, hoping it would shock some sense back into his system.

He couldn't believe he'd faked being asleep. It was an act of cowardice, and he knew it. But, like she'd been doing since she'd first set foot on his property, Thalia had caught him off guard and he hadn't known how to react.

Yeah, he was exhausted. Driving into the yawning mouth of snow hell on four hours of sleep had taken everything he had and a whole bunch more. That was the problem. If he'd had a little in reserve, he wouldn't have been so weak with relief to see those flares that he'd had to let Hoss carry Thalia inside. He wouldn't have stumbled walking into his own house, his weakness on full display.

He sure as hell wouldn't have needed her to support him. He wouldn't have had to lean on her, or have gotten so light-headed that he'd been completely unable to pull away from her. Even if he'd wanted to, he hadn't been able to let go of her. If anything, he'd held her even tighter. He still didn't know how he'd managed to get on the couch in front of the fire. Unless she'd out-and-out carried him. At this point, he wasn't sure.

J.R. couldn't see much of his reflection in the dark interior of the bathroom, but he stared nonetheless. What the hell was wrong with him?

Thalia by his side had felt warm. Real.

Safe.

He'd felt safe with her arm around his waist, with his arm around her shoulders. So much so, he hadn't wanted that moment to end.

"Don't be an ass," he said to his faint reflection. All these unwanted feelings were the result of the late night and the dangerous afternoon. Thalia had never been someone he could trust. She could ruin his life and destroy everything he'd built. Hell, if the fight at the bar was any example, she'd already gotten a head start.

But.

Because there was a huge but, and it went back before the snow started falling. Back when she'd been in his kitchen, again. Back when she'd come to say goodbye. Back when she'd promised not to tell anyone where he was.

She was from Hollywood. She was a former actress. She worked for Levinson. There was no way he could trust her, not in this life and not in the next.

So when she'd been curled up at his side, one arm around his waist, her head resting on his shoulder, and whispered, "Thank you," in a voice he knew—felt deep in his soul—wasn't an act or a negotiating tactic…well, he'd frozen up. His brain had tried to tell him it was another trap, but the rest of him? The rest of him didn't know what it wanted.

Well, that wasn't true, either. Large parts of him wanted to hold her closer, to duck his head down and plant a gentle kiss on her lips. Then maybe another, not so gentle one.

Those kissing parts and his brain parts had canceled each other out, leaving him without a clear course of action. So he'd faked it.

He heard footsteps overhead. The bathroom was tucked

under the stairs, so that meant someone was coming back down. He finished his business and headed out. He was going to bed good and early, but he wasn't about to miss dinner. Not if Thalia was there.

Hoss was throwing a few more logs on the fire; Minnie was peeking into the oven. Weather like this was one of the reasons they had a gas stove—if they got truly desperate, they'd turn on the oven to heat the room. In many ways, this was a normal night. Except for the blizzard and the woman who was still upstairs.

"She gone to bed?" he asked, hoping she had and also hoping she hadn't.

"No, getting her things put away," Minnie said as she got out the plates. "We'll eat in front of the fire, if that's okay with you."

"Sure." Normally, she wouldn't have asked. When they lost power in the winter, they always pulled the couch and chairs up close to the fire and took their meals there. Most of the time, they all slept down here, too, so there'd only be one fire going. But she was going to be upstairs, someone had to be up there with her, just in case. In case of what, he wasn't sure, but he didn't think it would be best for her to be all alone upstairs in the middle of a blizzard. He should stay in his room. He'd be down the hall.

This was what Thalia did. She made things not normal. She made *him* not normal.

She came down a few minutes later. She'd changed—her other clothes were probably still wet from the snow. Hell, he should have gone up and changed his jeans. Too late now. She was here and the food was ready.

"Help yourselves," Minnie said, scooping the baked pork chops and wild rice onto a plate.

"You okay?" J.R. asked Thalia in a low voice. She looked okay—actually, she looked great—but something about her face had him worried.

She gave him a watery smile. "Just a long day. You? Have a good nap?"

He supposed he should be glad he could still pull off a little bit of acting, but it left a sour taste in his mouth. "Yup." Then he was handing her a plate and talking about how good the chops smelled and having dinner with her.

And the funny thing was, it all felt perfectly normal. Which meant it wasn't.

By the time the two of them got back to the fire, Minnie and Hoss had taken the chairs. What was this—a conspiracy? J.R. took a seat on the couch and waited. Would Thalia sit close enough to touch, or would she crowd into the far side of the couch, closest to Minnie?

She split the difference. If he wanted to, he could lean over and elbow her. Which would be rude. At least Minnie wasn't giving him the stink eye this go-round.

Instead, the whole meal was easy. Thalia asked questions about blizzards, J.R. answered, Hoss told stories that scared the hell out of her and Minnie did the reassuring.

At no point did she start talking about movies or Oscars or James Robert Bradley. She didn't treat him like he was special or anything. She treated him like, well, a friend. A friend she'd go into a bar and have a drink with. A friend she'd eat dinner with.

He was almost having fun—more fun than the first meal they'd shared. Especially when she looked at him—which she did a lot. They weren't that far apart. Just a few feet and some forks and knives separated them. The firelight threw a warm glow across her face, and her grin was deep and honest.

They were stuck here for a week, maybe two. He couldn't pretend to be asleep the whole time. What was he going to do?

By the end of the meal, Thalia was trying to politely hide her yawns behind her hand. J.R. was too tired to even make that effort.

"Can I help with the dishes?" Thalia asked Minnie.

"Heavens, no." Minnie chuckled, although she was clearly pleased with the offer. "We pile them into the sink until the water heater is heating again. You go on up to bed." She gave J.R. one of her motherly looks that spoke louder than words.

Yeah, he probably looked like hell and he was in serious danger of passing out and drooling on the coffee table. "I'm going to hit the hay, too."

"You all holler—loudly—if you need anything." Already wrapped in a buffalo robe, Hoss's Lakota accent was stronger, his eyes half-closed as he stared at the fire.

J.R. knew he and Minnie would stay up half the night, telling the old Lakota legends and long-ago family stories while they kept the fire going. He'd learned a lot the first couple of winters out here, like how Hoss's father had died in a car wreck when he was a little boy and how Minnie had been raised by her grandma, who barely spoke English.

"Good night, all." Thalia looked at him as she stood, and he had to fight the urge to take her hand in his and lead her upstairs to a bedroom. Maybe hers, maybe his. Did it matter?

Damn, but he must be tired to be thinking like that. Instead, he stood and grabbed the flashlight. That was a safer option, by far.

They climbed the stairs in silence. He knew he needed to get into his room and shut the door—the sooner the better. Bolting on her would be rude, all the more so since he had the flashlight. He should make sure she was okay in her room. That was the polite, gentlemanly thing to do.

The hall was dark, but the blowing snow cast a pallid white glow over everything. In the light, Thalia's eyes looked huge. And something else. Was she scared? "It'll be fine," he said as he stood in the hall.

She nodded, but didn't say anything, which made him feel like he had to say something else. "My room is right there, so if you need anything…"

Maybe that wasn't the right thing to say? He'd messed it

up somehow, because she dropped her gaze to the floor and managed to look embarrassed.

"J.R.—" she began, and he knew she was going to try and thank him again. And he knew if she did, he'd want to kiss her again. And that would be a problem. Although, honestly, he was so tired he was having trouble remembering why that would be a problem, but he knew it would mess things up. Everything he'd built for himself would be in danger if he did something foolhardy like pursue his attraction to Thalia Thorne.

So he interrupted her with, "Yeah, knock if you need something. I'll see you in the morning. 'Night."

He was a grown man, by God, and as such, he did not sprint down the hallway to avoid uncomfortable conversations with a woman.

But he walked quickly.

Nine

That was...odd.

Thalia changed into her flannel jammies, threw another log onto the fire and climbed underneath what felt like twenty quilts and blankets.

J.R. had just...left her standing outside her door. The man had risked his life for her, but he acted like he didn't want her to thank him. If she didn't know better, she'd think he was almost afraid of her.

Which was ridiculous. He'd taken on that cowboy in the bar at the drop of hat and driven into a blizzard. He couldn't be afraid of her. Could he?

She was the one being ridiculous. What had she expected him to do? Stand there while she gushed over him? This wasn't Hollywood, and whatever he'd once been, he wasn't the kind of man whose ego needed constant reassurance.

Ugh. She was stressed and tired and all-over confused. Overthinking right now would be as productive as chasing her tail. She'd go nowhere but in circles.

She curled into a ball under all the bedding, wishing she could feel her toes more than she could now. The fire made a huge difference. The room was easily twenty degrees warmer than the stairwell and the hall. She certainly wouldn't freeze to death. That didn't make it *warm*.

Thinking about J.R.'s arm around her shoulders, though—yeah, there was a little heat there. Her mind played over the moment when he'd kissed her forehead in the car. It hadn't been a hot 'n' bothered kind of kiss, but somehow, the tenderness of it left her with a distinctly bothered feeling. He'd come close to kissing her on three different occasions now. Was she going to have to settle for a single touch of his lips when he was right across the hall?

At least the tossing and turning she was doing helped keep her warm.

Thalia slipped in and out of sleep. The fire had a mesmerizing quality to it, and she wasn't sure if she was dreaming some of the shadows it threw or not. Time seemed to have stopped. There was no day or night, no dark or light. Just white snow and red fire, a comfy bed and cold toes, and the man across the hall that she'd always wanted.

She thought about her life, her mother and what waited for her back in Hollywood. She thought about *Blood for Roses,* the movie she wouldn't get to make. It would have been a great movie, too.

At one point, Thalia knew she was dreaming because she was watching *Hell for Leather* in the theater with her college boyfriend, the one she'd left behind when she moved to Hollywood. That date had happened a long time ago, but sitting in the dark theater felt real. James Robert's amber eyes jumped off the big screen and seared themselves on to her heart. Breathless, she watched him ride across the range, his six-shooter firing with deadly accuracy. God, how she'd loved that role, that movie. That actor. She'd seen all of his movies, but this one—with him scruffy and rugged and way more than a little dangerous—this was the one that put her past schoolgirl crush and right over into borderline obsession.

Then the scene changed, and James Robert was in a cabin in front of a roaring fire, leaning against the mantle. The firelight made his hair shine like gold in the dark room, but he seemed worried.

Wait, Thalia thought. *Was that scene in the movie?* No, she'd remember it. She'd seen *Hell for Leather* enough to have the whole thing memorized.

She pushed herself up, but the scene didn't change. He was standing in her room, wearing green-and-blue-plaid flannel pajama bottoms under a thick green bathrobe. "J.R.?"

"My fire went out." His voice—no way she was dreaming. "I wanted to be sure yours was still going."

"Oh." For some reason, this disappointed her. "Are you cold?"

He shrugged, but that was the only answer she got. He hadn't even looked at her, as if he was afraid she was sleeping in the nude and he was violating her privacy by being here.

"You're cold." It wasn't a question anymore, just a statement of fact. His fire went out—so he checked on her. He'd put her first, again.

"Used to it." His voice sounded like he'd been gargling with gravel.

Thalia swallowed. Was she sure she wasn't dreaming J.R. here, in her room, almost close enough to touch? Oh, how she wanted to touch him, to feel his work-roughened hands on her body. Then she remembered how he'd bolted in the hallway. Right. Throwing herself at his feet was out. That didn't mean he had to leave. "You can stay in here, if you want."

Even though he didn't move, everything about him tensed. She half thought he was going to break the mantle off the wall. "I'll go."

"No, stay. At least long enough to warm up." Let me warm you up, she wanted to say, but the last thing she wanted was for him to accuse her of trying to seduce him for the wrong reasons.

She thought he was going to leave, but instead he sat cross-legged on the floor. "Until I warm up."

He didn't look like he was planning on sleeping. Something about this situation felt a little like the conversation they'd had on the phone last night, except this time, the distance between them was only a few feet. With him sitting so close to her, everything about him looking rugged and scruffy, she didn't think she'd be able to sleep anytime soon. What she wouldn't give to slide her arm around his waist like she had earlier, to feel his weight against her. What she wouldn't give for that moment of connection. "Why did you leave?"

Without looking away from the fire, he said, "I hated it so much. *So* much. I couldn't buy a grapefruit without someone taking pictures of me. They made fun of my clothes, my body, my everything." She saw him grin, but it was a joyless thing.

"People made fun of you? But everything I read about you was always so glowing. You were such a golden boy—so perfect."

This time, his grin seemed more real. "You read those things, did you? Or was that for research?"

"I've seen all the James Robert Bradley movies." Revealing that felt dangerous, like when she'd called him from her room. She was crossing another line that couldn't be uncrossed.

"All of them? Even *Babydoll Smile?*"

That had been one of those teen sex romps from early in his career. "Even *Babydoll Smile.* Which was terrible, I might add."

His grin widened as he tucked his knees under his chin. He didn't seem to be as cold, but she thought she saw him shiver. His back was probably freezing. "I was fully capable of bad acting. Which begs the question, Thalia. Why do you want me for your movie?"

And just when she thought things were lightening up. This was the price she paid for crossing that small line moments ago. He knew now. She thought about trying to fudge the truth, but then he said, "And don't feed me that line about how 'people' want to know and will pay, either. I think I've earned an honest answer."

He had, darn it all. She owed him the truth. Taking a deep breath, she forced herself to look at the fire. That made confessing seem less...intimate. "It was me. *I* wanted to know what happened to you." He didn't say anything, which somehow made her jumpier, so she kept talking. "You were the reason I wanted to become an actress. It sounds crazy, but..." the words, *I had the biggest crush on you* refused to actually move past her back teeth. So she hedged, hoping to turn the conversation back to him. "You'd left by the time I hit town. I missed you by months. You didn't even come back to award the Best Supporting Actress Oscar the next year. You were *gone*."

Which was a lousy thing to say—like she was mad he hadn't waited in Hollywood for her arrival. But if he kept asking her questions and she kept answering them honestly, she had no idea if she would even be able to look him in the face in the morning.

"That's the thing I don't understand about you." Every part of Thalia tensed up at this broad statement. What on Earth was he going to say? That she was some kind of nut? That she was delusional? That she'd always be a nobody? Levinson had said all those things to her, and more.

But J.R. wouldn't, a fact he illustrated when he went on. "Anyone who's ever found out about James Robert Bradley has forgotten about me. It's like I cease to exist." She could hear the hurt in his voice, could guess that more than a few women had broken the heart of the man sitting before her.

"You're different. You already knew about all that, and you still…" He turned his head to her, meeting her gaze from across the room. Head on his knees, he was curled into an impossibly small ball. Despite the massive strength displayed by his broad shoulders, she saw the little boy who'd wanted to be a firefighter, army man, astronaut and a cowboy. But never an actor. "You still treat me like I'm a real person."

The way he was looking at her did a lot to raise her personal temperature. Her heart about stopped, although she couldn't tell if that was from the heartbreak behind his statement or from the best compliment she'd ever received. She had no idea how to reply without sounding like a doofus. "You are real. To me."

The corner of his mouth crooked up—not much, but a little. The firelight lit his face from the side, bathing him in the glow of warmth. *Oh,* she thought, *that's the real smile.* The one that could melt her in the middle of a blizzard.

Then she saw a shiver shake his body, and he began to rub his shins for warmth. "Are you still cold?"

"It's fine."

Whatever moment they'd shared felt distant already.

"It's not." She'd seen movies with blizzards in them. As far as she could tell from that limited pop-culture selection, the way people kept warm when they were freezing to death was through body heat. "Come get under the covers." She hoped that came out in a no-nonsense tone, not a swoony, seductive tone. But she couldn't tell.

His eyes squeezed shut and it looked like he was gritting his teeth, like he was undergoing new and cruel mental tortures. "I'll be fine."

She had about enough of this tough-guy thing he was working. He was probably two steps from hypothermia. She was not about to let him walk out of here. She wouldn't touch him, she promised herself. She wouldn't give him a reason to think she was trying to seduce him for ulterior motives. This was entirely innocent.

Well, maybe not entirely. To be under the covers with J.R.? Somehow, that was even more exciting than the thought of sleeping with James Robert Bradley.

She tossed off the blankets and got out of bed. Even though she had socks on, the moment her feet hit the floor, the cold jolted her fully awake. And he'd been sitting on that? Heavens. Forcing a stoic J.R. into her bed wasn't exactly a dream come true, but she wasn't going to let him turn into a Popsicle to preserve his male pride.

She managed to get hold of his arm before he got to the door. "No, you're going to warm up. Come to bed."

He met her eyes, and the temperature in the room kicked up several notches. "It would be best for *both* of us if I go back to my room."

"No, it won't." She didn't know which part would keep her up more—the thought of him freezing to death, or the memory of the way he had looked at her. Either way, she wasn't sleeping. "And this isn't about sex," she added, more to remind herself than him. She wasn't doing a single thing to make him think this was a calculated negotiating tactic. Including doing exactly what she wanted with him. "This is about warmth."

"Thalia—" he said, his voice sounding deeper now. More dangerous. And much, much warmer.

She was playing with fire, but she couldn't let him see how much he was affecting her. She shoved him toward the mountains of blankets. "You're not leaving this room until you have a regular body temperature."

He stood at the side of the bed, the firelight shining in his eyes. Her breath caught in her throat, and she managed to avoid sighing in satisfaction. "This is about warmth."

"Yes." The way it came out—as a squeak—completely contradicted the words, but she refused to look away. "Just warmth." That and long-held, deeply personal fantasies. She wasn't going to let him know that. Not now, not ever.

He stood there, his gaze blazing down on her until she was sure she was going to crack. Then kicking off his slippers, he removed the bathrobe and spread it out on top of the blankets before climbing in. He scooted over and held the blankets up for Thalia to follow. Once she'd tucked the covers back up around her chin, she couldn't help but notice he was almost hanging off the other side of the bed. "For warmth." He sounded like he was speaking through clamped jaws.

"J.R., would you shut up?" Thalia rolled over to him and slid her arm around his waist, pulling him into her. Okay, so she'd immediately broken her no-touching rule. This wasn't any different than the way they'd been touching earlier, on the couch. So it was practically the same. Except for the fact that they were alone, in bed. There was that. "You've done nothing but take care of me. You beat that jerk up for me. You drove off into a blizzard for me. You have risked your life for me more times in the last few days than anyone else has in years. Decades. So you're going to let me return the favor, okay? I'm going to take care of you."

His eyes glittered. It would be so easy to push him over the edge, to take what they both wanted. But she didn't want him to think she was trying to trap him into something—into a stupid movie role. She swallowed, forcing her desire back and trying to dredge up some reason—any reason would do—that she was not seducing him. "Do you know how bad it would look if you froze to death because of me? I want to make sure you're warm."

Because he wasn't. He radiated chill through her jammies. She didn't know if she could warm him up or if he would freeze her out first.

He exhaled, then his opposite hand reached up and rested on her forearm. She fought the urge to throw her leg over his—to warm him up a little faster. It had nothing with wanting to melt into him, or wanting him to pull her in closer. Nothing at all.

Damn, he was *cold.* "It's just…" His voice was low, and close to her ear. If she closed her eyes, she could pretend this was pillow talk. "You being here makes things hard on me."

She leaned back enough to meet his eyes. The raw honesty she saw there came close to breaking her heart. "I'm not trying to make things hard." Then she realized what she'd said and her cheeks flushed hot. Which wasn't a bad thing, but the temperature under the blankets edged up again.

"I know." He moved his hand up and brushed freezing fingertips down her cheek. She shivered, but she didn't know if that was from the cold or the touch. "But you…"

Suddenly, she was the shy one, afraid of what he was going to say. Because she didn't know and couldn't guess. "Get some sleep," she said, but she couldn't help herself. She pressed his hand against her cheek and then turned her face to kiss his palm. So she'd said she wasn't going to seduce him. No more than she already had, apparently.

No, he'd been as good as his word. She had to do the same. Never mind that she was actually in bed with the former James Robert Bradley. Never mind that she'd lusted after him for a span of years that veered toward decades. Never mind that, as soon as this blizzard was a memory, she wouldn't see him again. Never freaking *mind* that this would be her one and only chance to make a long-held wish come true.

She'd loved an act, for that's all James Robert Bradley had been. That realization made her feel silly. The man in her arms wasn't some creation. He was real.

She forced herself to roll over and face the fire. After a few seconds, J.R. rolled with her, sliding one arm under her neck and the other around her waist. He pulled her back into the hard planes of his chest. This—this feeling of his body along hers, this close contact—this was what she wanted, but it wasn't, too. It wasn't enough.

"I'm glad you're here," he whispered in her ear. Then, moments later, his grip loosened and his chest rose and fell. *Get some sleep,* she told herself. As if that were possible.

Ten

Thalia did manage to drift off. After a while, J.R. stopped sucking all her body heat away from her and started to return the favor. She fell asleep feeling warm and secure in his arms. No matter what happened after this, she'd always have this sweet memory of lying in his arms. Even if that was as good as it got, it was still pretty damn good.

Lost in a dreamless fog, though, something changed. Heat coursed through her body—the kind of heat no fire, no amount of blankets, could match. She knew she was dreaming—she had to be, right? When she shifted, the pressure against her breast grew, focusing her desire.

Her eyes snapped open. Nope, not dreaming—J.R.'s hand covered her right breast and his other hand had drifted down to her hip bone. She wouldn't have thought it possible, but he'd pulled her into an even deeper embrace, and she could feel the hard length of him pressing against her backside.

He let out a little moan, his hot breath hitting her on the side of the neck and racing its way under the covers and down her back. She thought he was awake but then his hands jerked against her body, and she realized he was completely, totally, asleep. While palming her breast.

She'd think this whole situation funny, except he was turning her on. It'd been, what? A year since her last attempt at dating someone who worked in the entertainment industry? And like most of her relationships, this one had failed when Thalia had been unable—and, honestly, unwilling—to get the wannabe screenwriter's script in front of Levinson's eyes. She hated the feeling that even intimate relationships in Hollywood were predicated on favors.

J.R. shuddered, pouring more steamy breath onto her skin while digging his fingers into her body. He wasn't pawing her, but it was close, and the primal feeling of it—that even in sleep, he couldn't keep his hands off her—made her feel wanted in a basic, feminine kind of way.

And she wanted him back. She'd thought she'd lusted after James Robert the famous actor, but that juvenile emotion seemed pitiful compared to how much she wanted J.R., the real-life cowboy.

Moving slowly, so as not to disturb him, she covered his hand with hers, pressing it against her breast. His fingers were calloused, and she let hers drift over their roughness. Not the hands of a guy who had biweekly maintenance manicures, but the hands of a man who worked for a living.

The hands of a man who knew how to use them.

The thought of those hands moving over other bare parts of her body sent a shiver through her that had nothing to do with cold. She was on thin ice, that she knew. He'd expressly stated he wasn't here for her in the physical sense. His every move had shown he was here for her in the emotional sense, which was almost as big a turn-on as the thought of his body moving against hers. This was no teenaged crush, and it wasn't sheer lust. This was something different. Something special.

Except for the obvious fact that he was still out like a light and she was burning with desire. That was something of a problem.

Well, part of him was burning with desire, even if he wasn't consciously aware of it. With each shudder, each jolt, the hard length of him pressed against her with a more demanding need.

When he jerked again, the stubble of his beard scraped against the back of her neck, and Thalia couldn't bite back the low moan. Sex in Hollywood was a matter of power and negotiation, true, but it was also a competition—who had the better body, who had the better wax job, who had the money to pay for all that upkeep. The feeling of his facial hair on her bare skin was so raw, so real, that she couldn't help but grind her hips back into him. When was the last time she'd been *this* turned on?

What she wouldn't give to have fewer layers of flannel between them. *What the hell,* she thought. She wanted him. Actually, by this point, it had gone beyond mere "want" and had skipped straight on over into "need." She didn't just need the release of a good, old-fashioned orgasm. She needed to feel desirable. She needed to feel wanted. She needed *him.*

She lifted her free hand back and rested it on his hip, pulling him against her as she shimmied against him. Another moan escaped her lips.

This time, it wasn't quiet enough. J.R. stilled behind her, and she felt tension roll off him.

All the lines she'd crossed before were small, nearly invisible ones. But when she slipped her other hand down between their bodies and felt for herself how rock hard he was, she knew she was crossing the big, blinking line. She couldn't stop herself. The thing was, she had no idea if he would stop her or not.

She didn't want him to stop her. "I want you, J.R. *So*

much." To emphasize that, she formed his fingers around her breast while she traced his generous length again.

His breaths came so quick and fast that in seconds, he was panting. She tilted her head over her shoulder and managed to catch his cheek with her lips. When she did, he shuddered. She felt his body envelop hers as his lips moved against her neck. The stubble scraped over her skin, and she had to bite back another moan as he said, "I don't have anything."

"I'm on the Pill. Clean bill of health." She let go of his hand long enough to pull her shirt up, and when he placed all those calluses back on her bare nipple, she sucked in air. "You've taken care of me, J.R. Let me take care of you. All of you," she added as she rubbed against him.

For a painful, erotic second, he didn't say anything. Then he lowered his head and kissed the spot below her ear.

The relief that coursed through Thalia's body was immediate and intense, which only amplified the desire racing roughshod over her body.

They didn't speak another word. They didn't have to. She slipped her hand beneath the waistband of his pants and wrapped her fingers around the whole of him. The groan she was rewarded with spoke louder than any sweet talk could have.

When he returned the favor, sliding his hand below her waistband and rubbing those calloused hands over her most sensitive spot, she had to fight to keep what little control she had. He must have sensed how close she already was, because he used his chin to shove the shoulder of her top away and then took a nip at the bare flesh he'd exposed while stroking her harder and harder.

Wait, she wanted to tell him. She wanted to wait for him— but he didn't give her a choice. One set of calluses slid deeper into the folds of her body, rubbing with exquisite precision, while the other pulled and tugged at her nipple. The release crashed over her so hard, so fast, that she almost fell off the bed when her back arched.

He held on to her, pulling her back into him. "Whoa," was all he said, as if she were a young filly trying to buck him off, but she heard the satisfaction in his voice.

Yeah, whoa. Not since the fumbling days of her first serious boyfriend had a man taken the time to put her first. And just when she thought J.R. couldn't turn her on any more than she already was, too.

He held her as the last of the orgasm shuddered through her body, kissing her neck the whole time. If she were with some manscaped guy in Hollywood, he'd already be looking for affirmation that only he gave her that kind of climax, that he was the best she'd ever been with.

Not J.R. Instead, he made a low sound, deep in the back of his throat that sounded like pure happiness. Well, she could make him happier. She stretched back, trying to get a hold of him again.

"Whoa," he said again as he grabbed her hand. Then he was pulling her bottoms down, then his bottoms down, and finally, *finally,* no flannel stood between them.

She twisted so she could get the one thing she'd been missing—a kiss. "J.R.," she whispered, then his mouth covered hers. Their tongues tangled as his beard abraded her lips. *Primal*—that was the word. Something basic in her responded, sending heat rushing down between her legs and making her angle her backside for him. She threw her top leg over his, opening for him.

He lifted her off the bed, then he was against her, then he was sliding all of that length into her. He'd revved up her engine so much her body offered no resistance to what felt like an impressive size. With two concentrated thrusts, he was buried deep inside her.

When he paused, she cried out in protest. "J.R., *please.*"

"I want to feel you for a minute." But he shifted, lowering her upper body back down onto the bed and sliding his hand down her belly again.

Man, how she loved the feel of those rough calluses sliding over her. "Smooth," he murmured as he skimmed over the area she felt compelled to keep waxed even when she wasn't seeing anyone.

Before she could offer a comment, though, his fingers delved deeper, and suddenly he was thrusting and rubbing and tweaking her nipple and Thalia had no words. None. All she could do was hold on to his thigh, his arm, and lean back for quick, hot kisses as he drove into her again and again.

He licked at her neck and shoulder, rubbing his beard over her exposed skin. The rough sensation left scorch marks of heat on her skin. She lifted her hand behind his head and laced her fingers into his hair, holding his face against her neck.

He nipped her there, which drew a ragged gasp from her. Taking that as the sign of approval it was, he bit with more pressure.

Thalia came—hard. Her body tightened around him, *against* him, as the pleasure of being consumed ran roughshod over her body. He stopped thrusting as she rode it out, instead focusing on touching all of her spots with just the right amount of pressure. *Oh, so good* was all the conscious thought Thalia was capable of thinking. As the climax ebbed, she melted back into his body, grinning like a fool and wondering if she'd be the same again.

J.R. took his cue and ran with it. He rolled toward her, putting his hands on her hips and thrusting deeper, longer and harder. He wasn't holding back—no, he was giving her everything he had, and maybe a little something extra. She had to brace herself against the edge of the bed so she didn't fall off, but she didn't care. There was something so heated, so fierce about this act between them. She had no idea how she'd ever be happy with any of the metrosexuals back in L.A. ever again. Nothing and no one could compare to her cowboy.

With a groan that started deep in his chest and rumbled into a low roar, he thrust one final time and held. A smaller, delicious orgasm peaked in Thalia just from knowing she'd satisfied him as much as he'd satisfied her.

Wow. Even in all her fantasies of a wild night with James Robert Bradley, she didn't think that she'd gotten even close to the hottest spooning sex she'd ever had. What made it even better was that it wasn't the one-night stand she'd envisioned, where he barely remembered her name.

He fell back panting, but before she could do much of anything, he was running his fingertips over her shoulder, the part where he'd bit her. "I marked you," he said in a kind of surprised tone of voice. "I'm sorry."

She rolled over, throwing her arms around him. He fell onto his back, but he held her close. "Don't be." How could she tell him he'd marked her long before they had ever met?

What happened next? She'd had dates that ended in bed—and then ended, dates she thought had potential to be more than a one-night stand, but weren't. Would he treat her like she was a dime a dozen when they left this bed? Would things be weird down in the kitchen in the morning—weirder if Hoss and Minnie figured out what had happened?

Swallowing down her anxiety, she said, "Now what?" in a carefully moderated tone.

"Well," he replied with a hearty yawn, "I'm going back to sleep." Thalia's heart sank a little at that pronouncement. Maybe she'd deluded herself into thinking he cared about her. Then he tightened his arms around her and said, "I want to make sure I'm holding you, all the same." He yawned again. Yeah, maybe the sex had been…demanding. "'Night, Thalia. Again."

Oh. *Oh.* Thalia relaxed in the warmth of his embrace. "'Night, J.R."

She knew, without a doubt, that he knew who she was. Someone real.

Eleven

When J.R. opened his eyes, he could see it was lighter out. The tip of his nose was still cold, which meant Hoss hadn't gotten the generators going yet. Still no power. He had no idea what time it was. He'd headed upstairs probably around seven, but had been awake a lot throughout the night. It could be seven in the morning, could be ten. All he knew was he hadn't slept this late since, well, the last blizzard.

He'd been alone and cold then. Now? Excepting the tip of his nose, he was warm and happy. It felt a little unreal. The smell of femininity and sex that seemed infused into the covers around him was definitely unusual.

Sighing with contentment, he stretched as much as he could without disturbing Thalia. *Thalia.* She had his arm pinned under her head, but she'd rolled onto her back. Her mouth was open, and her hair was a wild mess. She looked exactly like a woman who'd been satisfied in bed. He didn't think she'd ever looked prettier.

He'd like to stay right here in this bed, too, but he was getting that twitchy feeling he always got when he slept much past six in the morning. Life on the ranch was early to bed, early to rise. By his second summer of getting up at 3:30 a.m. to work cattle before the heat hit, he'd gotten used to it. Which was fine, except on days like this. Sleeping in wasn't his style.

Part of him wanted to wake her with a kiss and a whole lot more, but the other part of him—the rational part—knew he couldn't delay the start to the day any longer. He had to get out to the barn, get the gas for the generator and see to his horses. If the wind had compacted the snow enough, he'd try to get out to the pastures on the snowmobile and check on the cattle. He loved that sort of thing, doing real work with his hands. It was night and day from what his life had been in Hollywood, where he worked and worked and never felt like he did anything. Nothing of value, anyway.

So this morning would have to wait. Until this evening. He just had to make it twelve hours. He could do that, right?

Yeah, right, he thought as he brushed a strand of hair off Thalia's cheek. Her eyelids fluttered as she turned her face toward him. "Hmmm," she all but purred. "Time to get up?"

"Yup." Part of him was already up, but he was going to exhibit the restraint that had abandoned him last night if it killed him. Which it might. He hadn't meant to wind up in her bed, in her arms—part of his brain still wasn't sure she wasn't using sex to get him signed to the part. But he wasn't going to listen to that part of his brain. Not today.

Eyes still closed, she smiled and touched his face, rubbing her fingertips over his facial hair. He was starting to think she liked the beard. A lot. "Five more minutes."

That was an option—nah, he decided. He didn't want to rush things with her. Tonight, he could take his time. "How about I get you some coffee?"

One eyelid popped up. "Did you just offer to bring me coffee? In bed?"

The way she said it made it pretty clear that no one had

ever made such an offer to her before. Which seemed a crying shame. Had no one ever taken care of her? "I'll be back in five minutes," he promised, but not before giving her the kind of kiss that made his evening plans clear.

"Mmmm." That time, she did purr. Damn, but she was making it hard to get out of this bed.

He managed to extricate himself from her body and the covers. The fire was down to straggling embers, so he tied his bathrobe and threw a few logs onto the coals. His slippers were cold, but the sheepskin lining was far warmer than the bare floor. "Be right back," he said, as if he was afraid she would bail in the amount of time it would take him to get downstairs and back up. Actually, he was a little nervous, but it wasn't like she could up and leave.

"Better be," she called out as he shut the door.

J.R. grinned the whole way down. For a long time—too long—his relationships with women had always proved true the famous line by Rita Hayworth—"Men go to bed with Gilda—they wake up with me." Women went to bed with James Robert; they didn't want to wake up with J.R.

Except for Thalia. She was different, which was something of a gross understatement. Even though she knew all about James Robert—and, from the sound of it, had harbored a huge crush on him—she seemed to want J.R.

She seemed to like him. Especially the beard.

Lost in this train of thought, J.R. entered the kitchen. Minnie stood at the stove, frying bacon and a mess of eggs. The smell of biscuits had his stomach rumbling something fierce. He glanced over to where Hoss was still wrapped up in his buffalo robe. Didn't look like he'd moved since last night.

"Morning, Minnie," he said with another yawn. "What time is it?"

"Nigh on to ten in the morning. Coffee's ready." She dusted flour off her hands before pointing to two thermal mugs with lids set on the counter.

"I'll take Thalia hers," he said, trying to keep his tone un-committed. Suddenly, he was nervous all over again—but not because of the possibility Thalia would bail. Because he hadn't given a moment's thought to what Minnie and Hoss would say, how they would treat this new development.

Minnie came up to him and touched him on the arm. "J.R.," she said, and he saw the worry in her eyes. *Are you okay?* she seemed to ask him with a look.

After all this time, it still made him feel good that Minnie cared. He remembered the first time he met her. Hoss had dragged him home from dinner after shooting one day, tell-ing him he couldn't live on beer and peanuts. J.R. had been braced for the gushing to start the moment Hoss's truck had stopped in front of the beat-up trailer an hour away from the movie set. That's what had always happened before. But from the moment Minnie had emerged from the trailer, a scold on her lips, he'd *felt* that she was nothing like his mother and nothing like the girls who threw themselves at him. The trou-ble had been, he hadn't known how to act around a woman like Minnie Red Horse.

Luckily, she hadn't made it hard on him. Before he'd even gotten his hat off his head, she'd been *tsking* him. "Good lord and butter, look at you. When was the last time you ate a meal?" had been the first words out of her mouth, followed closely by, "Come in, come in."

And that had been it. The Red Horse house had been small and run-down; the food wasn't five-star anything. But Min-nie and Hoss had taken him in, made a place for him at their table, and for the first time in his life, made him feel nor-mal. *Real.* So much so that he almost hadn't even gone back to Hollywood after filming had ended. Minnie had been the one to convince him he had to honor his obligations then, but she'd made it clear he was welcome in their home anytime.

It had taken him another year and a half, plus the death of his mother, before he'd been able to untangle himself from his acting career. He might never have done it—might have slipped further into alcoholism and drugs, might have wound up dead by the time he was thirty—if he hadn't had those moments of profound normalcy at the Red Horse table.

He owed them everything. He could only hope that, by giving them a home and jobs, by making them his family, he had come close to repaying that debt of gratitude.

J.R. grinned, touching Minnie's furrowed brow. "You worry too much, you know?" *I'm good,* he thought, squeezing her hand. *It's good.*

For only the second time in his life, it was good.

"Oh." Swear to God, it looked like Minnie's eyes were welling up with actual, sentimental tears. "That's…nice." Then she spun away from him before any of those tears could spill over. Before he knew it, she had a wooden spoon in her hand and was waving it dangerously close to him. "See? I *told* you that woman wasn't a danger."

"You and your womanly, Indian-y intuition were right." J.R. poured the coffee and capped the mugs. Then he saw the kettle on the stove. "That for us?"

"Only if you can carry it all." Minnie handed him the oven mitt.

J.R. grabbed the kettle in one hand, the mugs in the other, and headed back upstairs. By no means was the awkwardness over with, but Minnie's stamp of approval added to his feeling of lightness.

Thalia was propped up in bed, the covers up to her chin. "You brought me coffee," she said in wonderment.

"And hot water. I'll pour some in your sink before I head back to my room."

She glanced up at him through sleepy lashes, but he could tell she wasn't that sleepy anymore. "Oh?"

"Been thinking," he went on, as casual as could be, while he headed back to her bathroom. "Might be better if you stay in my room tonight. Use less firewood that way."

Which was a nice, polite way of asking her to sleep with him. And also, to sleep with him. Sure, the sex had been great, but he wanted her to wake up in his arms again. He wanted that closeness, that touch.

He wanted her. Plain and simple.

"Well," she called out to him as he filled her sink with the warm water. "I certainly wouldn't want you to have to get out of bed to check on my fire again."

"Exactly." He caught sight of himself in the mirror, grinning his fool head off. How long would the snow keep her here? How long could they pretend to play house? A week, maybe longer. Wouldn't be long enough, but he'd take what he could get.

When he went back into the bedroom, he was happy to see she had a huge, silly grin on her face, too. A real smile, one that pulled on her muscles and would one day lead to laugh lines—not one of those vapid smiles most actors perfected to keep wrinkles at bay. "Minnie's got breakfast going, then Hoss and I'll try to get to the barn. If we can get the gas into the house, we can fire up the generator."

She nodded, sipping her coffee. "Sounds like fun."

She was teasing him. "No, fun is mucking a stall in sub-zero weather."

"I can help." The offer came out of nowhere, but she seemed entirely earnest.

"Muck the stalls?" She nodded, her eyes huge. "Really?"

"My grandpa made me clean the barn in exchange for going riding," she said. "I don't mind."

He was trying not to gape at her, but he wasn't doing a good job. She was full of surprises, no doubt. The good kind. How many women in Hollywood would offer to shovel manure—outdoors—in a blizzard? Maybe just this one. "We'll ask Minnie about getting you bundled, then."

"Great!"

J.R. was still shaking his head at this pronouncement ten

minutes later as he waited in the hall for Thalia to emerge from her room. He'd washed up, put on the layers of long underwear and sweaters, and was sipping the rest of his coffee. He could handle a cold house—more so if he had Thalia to help keep his bed warm—but he'd sure like to shower before nightfall, maybe trim the edges of his beard.

After several chilly minutes, she came out, bundled in what looked like two sweaters, mug in hand. "Ready?" she asked, holding out her other hand for him to take. Like it was the most normal thing in the world.

"Ready." Ready to face Hoss. Ready for the snow. Ready for anything with her by his side.

When they got downstairs, Hoss had moved. Now he was standing before the fire, stretching. "Morning, you two," he said without even looking at them. Maybe Minnie had already told him to play it cool—or risk the wrath of her spoon.

"Morning." Thalia looked confident, but he heard the waver in her voice.

"Thalia's going to be moving into my room tonight." She shot him a less-than-pleased look. So that probably wasn't the most eloquent way of phrasing things. If there was one thing he'd learned in the last decade, it was that getting things out in the open made it better on everyone.

Minnie and Hoss both paused, and Thalia's hand clamped down on his. Then Minnie said, "That's nice," in the same tone she'd used earlier, and Hoss added, "Use less firewood, eh?" and it was just that easy.

"Yup. She's going to help out in the barn this morning, so Minnie, if you could get her set up after breakfast, that'd be great."

Minnie and Hoss shared a look that, for the life of him, he couldn't read. Which was odd, as he'd lived with them for a long, long time. He let it ride. It was time for breakfast, after all, and he was hungry.

Without much more ado, Minnie set out breakfast and they

all dug in. Minnie and Thalia talked about the gear she'd need to borrow—snowshoes, coveralls, gloves and the like—while he and Hoss discussed the plan of attack. "If you can get to the gas tanks, Thalia will help me with the barn."

If Hoss doubted the wisdom of this plan, he didn't show it. Instead, chewing his way around another piece of bacon, he said, "If I get the generator going and you two take care of the barn, then you and I can get the snowmobiles out and see if there's anything to be done about the cattle."

"Deal." Getting the generator running—with the accompanying heat and hot water—was a top priority.

After breakfast, Minnie took Thalia upstairs while Hoss and J.R. suited up in the mudroom. The whole time, J.R. waited for Hoss to say something. No smart-ass comments, no waggling eyebrows came his way. "Think she can make it out to the barn?" was all he said.

J.R. thought back to the serious way she'd offered to help. Honestly, he didn't know if she could handle the snow, much less the barn. "I ain't gonna be the one to tell her she *can't* do it."

"That's probably the smart move," Hoss said. "Don't strike me as the kind of woman who listens to what other people tell her she can't do."

Even J.R. had to chuckle. "When you're right," he said as he clapped Hoss on the shoulder, "you're right."

Thalia stood in the garage, which was about the size of a barn and had half a forest of firewood stacked in it. Minnie hadn't been lying—they could heat the house for a month, easy.

"Steady," J.R. said as he kneeled before her.

Thalia balanced herself against the back of Minnie's SUV as J.R. buckled her boot-clad foot into a snowshoe. She felt like the little brother in that movie *A Christmas Story.* Between her regular clothes and the sweatshirts, sweatpants, coveralls, hat, gloves, goggles and four pairs of socks Minnie had swaddled her in—plus the huge boots J.R. was working around—she didn't think she could put her arms down.

"There's a rope that goes from the house to the barn," Hoss was saying as J.R.'s hands worked. She wished she could feel his touch, but there were too many damn layers between them. "Don't let go of the rope."

"Hold on to rope. Got it."

"There." J.R. stood up, which was a pretty impressive series of moves for a man who was also wearing snowshoes. "Ready?"

Thalia nodded, but she wasn't so sure anymore. Offering to help in the barn had seemed like a fun idea at the time, but that was before she'd been trussed up as if she were going to climb Mont Blanc.

"Here we go." From her perch back by the door that led to the kitchen, Minnie opened the garage door. The whole thing groaned, and Hoss and J.R. rushed to help shove it up.

The wall of snow on the other side was impressive. As in, terrifying. "How much did we get?" she heard herself say.

"Probably only a couple of feet," J.R. replied as he assessed the pile that was much closer to her head than her knees. "This is just a drift. Once we get to the other side…"

Hoss already had a shovel and was pushing the snow away. After a few minutes, Thalia could see the crystal-white world on the other side. Everything looked both softer—the corners of buildings were cushioned and rounded, the world blanketed in comfortable white—and harsher. The wind had blown the snow into severe, sculpted drifts more fitting for a modern art museum than the Montana wilderness.

J.R. gave Hoss a leg up to get over the snow. Then he motioned to Thalia. "Your turn." She swore she heard something close to a tease in his voice.

What, did he think she'd chicken out? Hell to the no. She squared her shoulders and clomped over to where he waited for her. She couldn't see much of anything about him—he had on a full ski mask and goggles—but she would bet money he was smiling at her. "Ready," she said, hoping she sounded more confident than she felt.

J.R. nodded his head, then picked her up and more or less hefted her through the opening Hoss had shoveled. One of her snowshoes caught on the edge and she lost any semblance of balance.

"Watch it." From beneath his mask, Hoss's easy drawl reached her ears as he caught her by the arm and got her upright on the snowshoes. "We've got to stop meeting like this, you know."

"Agreed."

Hoss guided her over to the rope and waited until she'd looped her arm around it before he went back and helped haul J.R. up.

The nice thing was, for the first time since she'd arrived in this state, she wasn't freezing her butt off outside. The many layers she had on made moving a new and interesting experience, but she only felt the wind on her face. Her toes were, for the time being, safe.

J.R. took the place in front of her, and Hoss brought up the rear. Slowly, the three of them made their way out to the largest of the three barns. For her first time in snowshoes, she did pretty well. She hoped, anyway. At least she didn't fall into either of the men and she didn't let go of the rope.

Getting into the barn was an exercise in falling with style—at least, Thalia hoped she fell off the drift and into J.R.'s waiting arms with style. He unbuckled her snowshoes for her and she stepped clear. "Wait here while we get the gas," he said.

Nodding, she looked around. The barn was massive. From where she stood, she could see a full-sized, covered arena behind a gate on her left. Straight ahead was a row of stalls—maybe twenty in all. Did he keep that many horses? Wow. To her right was a big room with a desk and a bunch of saddles on the wall—the tack room and office.

The whole place was clean and bright, with paint that looked relatively fresh on the walls and the smell of alfalfa hanging in the air. Thalia took a deep breath, smelling the scent of a childhood summer spent at Grandpa's farm.

She was hit with an unexpected burst of homesickness— not for Hollywood, but for Oklahoma. She'd been so busy with work that it had been hard to find the time to get home to see Mom and pay a visit to Grandpa's and Dad's graves. She'd been trying to tell herself she was going back when she had this project done, or that award—that Oscar—won, but maybe that hadn't been what had kept her away. Maybe it had been that she hadn't wanted to go home until she was as famous as her mother thought she was.

Thalia walked to the first stall. She hadn't lied to J.R.— she'd always loved horses and had mucked plenty of stalls in her day to earn an afternoon riding around Grandpa's land. She was less than thrilled to see it was empty.

So were the next four stalls on either side of the sawdust-covered aisle, which left her with a vague sense of unease. There were horses somewhere in here, right?

Then, in the fifth stall, she found one and, from the sound of it, the next several stalls were also filled. The horse in the stall—a dirty white gelding with a long mane that flopped every which way—nickered at her through the bars. She saw he had a quilted blue blanket over him. That was good. She didn't want to think the horses were out here freezing.

"Hello, baby," she murmured, pushing her goggles back and holding her hand out for the horse to sniff. "What's your name?"

"Coot," came a voice from behind her. "As in, Old Coot." Thalia turned to see J.R. standing, his legs spread wide as if he were master of everything in his domain.

She'd be lying if she said she didn't feel a little thrill of excitement at seeing him. He'd removed his mask and pushed his hood back, revealing his rugged face. "He's retired," J.R. added, coming up next to her and patting Coot on the neck. "We rode together for a long time, didn't we, Coot?"

Thalia once had known a lot about how horses worked. She would have thought she'd forgotten almost all that knowledge, but she was surprised by what kept bubbling up from deep in her memory. "And you keep him?" When Grandpa had retired horses, he'd sent them off to some other farm. Any animal on his farm had to earn his keep—like his granddaughter.

"We've been through a lot." J.R.'s voice was low as he scratched the old horse behind the ear. "He was the first horse I bought—taught me a lot about riding on the range. I feel better knowing he's here and taken care of." He turned a goofy grin to her, but his eyes weren't telling the same tale. "Sounds dumb, huh?"

"No." She didn't want to embarrass him—or herself—by telling him it was noble, sweet, thoughtful and touching. Instead, she rubbed Coot's nose and changed the subject. "You have a lot of empty stalls here. Where are all the horses?"

"We only keep the seven here. The rest of the stalls are for the hired help to use in the summer months." He slid open Coot's door and haltered him. "I usually let them out into the arena to run off some energy after a big storm. Get the gate?"

"Sure." She walked on the opposite side of Coot and swung the gate in for them.

J.R. led Coot into the center of the arena before he released his halter. The old horse didn't bolt, though. He stood there, sniffing J.R.'s face while J.R. rubbed his neck.

This, in a nutshell, was what made J.R. a good man—and a better man than James Robert probably ever was. He took care of his horse. Something about that said old-school cowboy, loyal and true. Thalia's heart swelled watching them. He could play the gruff cowboy, but this—a big smile on his face as he cooed to his favorite horse—was who he really was. And he trusted her enough to be that man in front of her.

J.R. sent Coot off at a leisurely trot, then went out a different door at the top of the arena. He reappeared carrying two bales of hay, one in each hand. Wow, Thalia thought, imagining all those muscles flexing underneath his coveralls. Strong, yet gentle. Tough, yet vulnerable.

She was forgetting all about her crush on James Robert. J.R. was so much better than her fantasy had ever been. *So much.*

"We'll put the grain in their stalls in a bit," he said by way of explanation after Thalia shut the gate behind him, even though she doubted Coot was a flight risk. The old guy had his nose buried in the first bale of hay, munching happily.

J.R. let her lead the next horse, a paint mare named Whipper. Whipper was only a few years old, and wasn't interested in communing with a strange woman while perfectly good hay was being eaten by Coot right over there. Thalia turned her loose and then had to step back to avoid the parting high kick Whipper threw at her on her way to the hay.

J.R. grinned at her from the gate. "Like I said, they've got a little energy to burn." It should have sounded like he was mocking her, but she thought she heard a compliment—which he confirmed when he added, "Nice move. A true greenhorn would have gotten kicked in the head."

"It's been a long time since I've gotten kicked." They were walking down the aisle toward the next horses to be turned loose. "I think I was riding Cinnamon, a little pony my grandfather kept for me. That stinker decided to jump a branch about a foot off the ground. I went down hard, and her back hoof clipped my calf on the way down."

"Aw, that don't hardly count. I took a horseshoe to the shoulder once, trying to get a rock out of Coot's hoof." He pointed to his right shoulder. "Hurt like a son of a…gun." Then he winked at her.

Next came Hoss's horse, Rabbit—"Because he hops when he trots," J.R. said—Mac, Gater and Yoda, a draft horse with massive ears and a wrinkled nose. "Hoss's doing," J.R. said by way of explanation as Thalia giggled at the name.

Then they were down to the last horse. J.R. hesitated before a stall, and as soon as she saw the horse, she knew why. The animal was a brilliant palomino, the warm color making his mane shimmer like spun silk. Thalia had seen him before, riding across the frozen land like he owned it. "This is…Oscar." The way he said it made it clear he was embarrassed. "This is my horse."

He'd named his horse Oscar. All this talk of not being an actor anymore, but he hadn't put it as far from him as he pretended he had. Thalia could only hope this Oscar loved him back. "Quite the golden boy, aren't you?" Oscar whinnied as he sniffed her hand, then moved his head back to J.R.

A ruddy blush was turning J.R. an unusual shade of red. He *was* embarrassed. "Hey." She grabbed him and pulled his head down to hers. "You don't have to be ashamed of that— of any of that. Not with me."

She brushed her lips over his, but he didn't kiss her back. His eyes were closed, and he looked like he was concentrating. She didn't know if that was a good sign or not.

"Thalia." As he said her name, he touched his forehead to hers. His arms went around her waist, pulling her in close. "About what I said earlier."

"Yeah?" He'd already apologized for asking if Levinson had assigned her to seduce him. What now?

"You…" He cleared his throat, his eyes still jammed shut. "You being here *does* make it hard on me. But you make it easy on me, too. And that's hard for a man like me to get used to."

Oh. *Oh.* She exhaled, struggling to keep her knees under her. That had to be the sweetest, most heartfelt thing a man had ever said to her. And she had no doubt he meant it, too. Every single word.

She kissed him. At first, the daylight kiss—with an equine audience—was stiff and awkward, but then she felt him relax into her as his tongue brushed her lips. The heat was there, but the barn wasn't exactly warm, and there was no way anything could be maneuvered through these layers. She broke the kiss and hugged him. The nice thing was, he hugged her back.

"Tonight?" Going to bed with him in his room, knowing he'd be there when she woke up in the morning—yeah, this could be easy. Nice and easy.

"Tonight," he agreed, the wide smile erasing any of his embarrassment. They got the last horse into the arena and then he got out the pitchforks.

They worked in silence, but she could see him watching her. Maybe he was waiting for some sort of reaction of disgust or horror? "You know, it's funny," she told him as she dumped another scoop into a wheelbarrow. "I'm pretty sure I've dealt with less crap here than in an average day in Hollywood."

He snorted in appreciation. "That, I don't doubt. Get back to me in a few more days."

"How long do you think we'll be here?"

"We've got a bulldozer—Hoss's baby. It'll take a week or two to plow out to the main road, and then it all depends on the roads." He paused, giving her a serious look. "We'll get you home one way or another."

Which was going to be a crying shame when it happened. Home, back to where Levinson would fire her, she'd be hard-pressed to find another job and she'd lose her apartment. Maybe it was wishful thinking, but she'd rather stay here, where horses played and fires—the wood kind and the personal kind—burned hot.

Thalia got lost in her thoughts as they cleaned the barn. He didn't know everything about her. He'd made his feelings about her boss, Levinson, crystal clear. How would he react to the fact that she'd had an affair with the man he detested so openly?

Badly, that's how. She hoped it wouldn't come to that, though. They'd have this brief time together, and then she'd be on her way and he'd never look at her with shock or disappointment. It wasn't lying, not exactly. Neither of them had brought up old lovers.

No, there was no room for Levinson in this…well, *relationship* was a strong word. This temporary weather situation. Whatever it was, Levinson had no place in J.R.'s bedroom or his barn.

As J.R. dumped the last wheelbarrowful, Thalia hung on the gate and watched the horses trot around. Yoda was playful for a horse as big as he was. He'd take a running start at Whipper and Rabbit, his plate-sized hooves taking huge divots out of the arena floor. Whipper and Rabbit would rear and whinny and bolt out of Yoda's reach, heels kicking the whole way. Then Yoda would stand there and nicker at them, clearly laughing at their melodramatic reactions.

Mac and Gater stood off to one side, scratching each other's back through the blankets every horse wore. Oscar trotted around the edge of the arena, keeping clear of the antics of the other horses. A creature apart, Thalia thought as he gave her a wide berth. Just like his rider.

Coot ambled up to her and blew snot on her outstretched hand. "Hey, you," she said as she scratched his head. The old boy's eyes fluttered shut as he leaned into her hand. "You like that?"

It had been years since she'd been on a horse, but she'd loved riding as a kid. Too bad she was stuck on a ranch in the middle of a blizzard. That sort of ruled out trail rides, and she couldn't say if she'd ever be out here again. And thinking that left her feeling morose.

"He likes you," J.R. said as he walked down the aisle pulling a bin of grain behind him.

"I was thinking how long it's been since I've ridden." She stood on her tiptoes to give Coot a behind-the-ear scratch.

"Yeah? How long?" He was farther down the aisle, dumping grain into buckets.

"Grandpa died during my ninth-grade year. Mom tried to hold on to the family farm, but…" It had been the hardest thing she'd ever seen her mother do. That farm had been in her family since the days of the Sooners. The day of the auction, when Thalia was a junior in high school, Mom had cried herself to sleep. "After we lost it, I felt like…I didn't have anything holding me to the state. Like I'd lost a piece of my family."

Coot sighed. *Yeah,* she thought as she smiled at the old guy. *That.*

"Your mom is still down there?" J.R. had come out of the stalls, his bin mostly empty.

"She is. Dad died a long time ago, but she's made a good life for herself. She was so mad at me when I dropped out of college to go to Hollywood because I was supposed to be the first one in the family to get a college degree. So she went back and got one instead. She works at the library, has a group of ladies she lunches with and seems happy." She still worried about her daughter and the subtle hints for grandchildren were less subtle every day. All in all, at the age of fifty-five, Thalia thought her mom had made peace with the hand Fate had dealt her.

"She loves you." Thalia could hear the wonder in J.R.'s voice.

"She does." Did that bother him, to know that other mothers loved their children and his mother hadn't—at least, not in the traditional way?

"The thing that's always been difficult for me to figure out is if my mother was more normal and Minnie is the crazy one, or if Minnie's normal and my mother…well, she *was* crazy." He shrugged, but didn't seem to be as anxious about such a blanket statement this time.

"I'd go with Minnie being the more normal of the two." She wanted to say her mother would be thrilled to meet him, but she knew that would imply that this whatever they had going right now would outlast the snow on the ground, and that would be a mistake. No matter how easy it was to spend the day petting horses and the night in his bed, she couldn't lose sight of the fact that everything about this was temporary, and sooner or later, the snow would melt.

So instead, she patted Coot on the neck and got the lead rope and started putting the horses back in the stalls, where they snarfed their grain down with great relish. She and J.R. put their goggles and snowshoes back on, and then he hefted her up the snowbank. She did better walking back to the house than she had before. *See?* She thought to herself as she slid back into the garage. *I'm not totally hopeless.* She hoped J.R. felt the same way.

When they got their snowshoes off, J.R. paused. "Listen," he said, a grin peeking out from his mask.

Thalia cocked her head to one side. At first, she didn't hear anything—but then she realized it wasn't silent. She could hear the faint sound of an engine running.

"Hoss got the generator fixed?"

"Yup." He took her hand and led her into the mudroom. The sound of a radio filled the kitchen, and Minnie was singing along.

"Oh, thank heavens." She certainly wasn't frozen stiff, but a hot shower was high on her to-do list. Especially if she was going to be spending the night with J.R. She grinned up at J.R., who gave her a squeeze. It was a small move, but—

given that Minnie was only feet away—it felt like this huge, almost-public declaration of togetherness.

Sheesh, she felt like she was in junior high again. What would happen if they got caught kissing?

Twelve

They got the snowmobiles up and running, and talking was impossible once they were streaking across an almost unrecognizable range. The snow had drifted over their heads in some spots. The going was cold and treacherous, and it required J.R.'s full attention. They couldn't even make it to the far north pasture. Might be a few more days before they could get hay out to the animals.

When they made it back to the barn, Hoss didn't say anything that wasn't directly related to cows, horses or food. Even then, he was uncharacteristically restrained. He was making J.R. nervous, plain and simple.

"She really help muck the barn?" was Hoss's big question.

"Yup." Which had been as much of a shock to J.R. as it was now to Hoss. He'd entertained the thought that her offer to shovel manure was one of those things some women did to convince a man they loved everything he did, but, when faced with actual crap, she'd try to talk her way out of it. Or at least pale and complain about the smell. But no, she'd shoveled like it was second nature. And, somehow, looked good doing it, snowsuit and all.

"Huh." Hoss scratched his nose, and J.R. braced himself for something inappropriate. "Wouldn't have figured she was the type."

"Nope," J.R. agreed, even thought it wasn't wholly clear which type Hoss was referring to—the type that mucked barns, or the type that J.R. fell into bed with.

Maybe both, as it had been a long time since he'd fallen into bed with anyone. In the past, he'd spend a lot of time trying to gauge how much his lady friend knew and how she'd react when she found out about James Robert Bradley. Dating had felt like a negotiation, as intense and demanding as any contract negotiation he'd ever been a part of. Every step had to be calculated for risk and damage control—an exhaustive process that left little for the actual courting of a beautiful woman.

For the last decade, dating had been hard. But Thalia knew all about James Robert, and she honestly didn't seem to care. Well, maybe she did care. But that wasn't the only thing she cared about. That's what made her different. He didn't have to hide that part of his life from her, and she wasn't going to hold it against him. She made it easy on him. He didn't have to do any of that negotiation stuff this time, which freed up his brain to think of a whole bunch of other fun stuff. Stuff that involved a crackling fire, a warm bed and a very naked Thalia.

Claiming he was cold, he pushed Hoss out of the barn. Low clouds scuttled across the gray sky, which meant they might have another couple of inches of snow on top of this fine mess in the morning. Normally, J.R. would be cursing the weather gods right about now.

He wasn't. All he knew was another few inches of snow meant another few days with Thalia. He couldn't remember looking forward to something so much in a long, long time.

When he and Hoss got into the house, Thalia had changed. She looked like she'd taken advantage of the hot water, and her hair was loose and long. Had she showered in his room? Without him? Man, it was warm in the house. Or maybe that was his personal temperature.

When she saw him, her eyes lit up so bright that he got hot just looking at her. "How was it?"

"Bad," he said, but he thought, *good.* Good, deep snow. The Department of Transportation didn't plow the twenty miles from the main road to his house. Hoss could dig them out, but that took time. The last time it had snowed this much, it had taken two weeks to get the drive plowed. The fact of the matter was that Thalia was his, all his. Odds were good she wouldn't be able to leave before Valentine's Day, which was a few weeks away.

He made his way over to her. Hoss and Minnie were doing their best to watch him without actually looking at him as he pulled Thalia into his chest and kissed her…forehead. *Damn,* he thought, feeling his face flush. Couldn't pull the trigger and seal the deal. But kissing Thalia in front of Minnie was too much like making out in front of a mom. It felt awkward.

"Have a good afternoon?" he said, more to cover his embarrassment than anything else.

Thalia's cheeks were pinking up, which made her glow. "Minnie managed to get the satellite up." The way she said it made it pretty clear she was used to 4G-broadband-whatever, and not the satellite connection they had to depend on way out here in the country. "And I was able to email my mom."

"Good." He was almost afraid to look at Minnie, but he'd be hard-pressed to say why. It wasn't like she would send him to his room without supper—or, like his mother would have done, threaten to kill herself if he ever left her. "And work?" What had she told Levinson?

Her grin turned sly. "I told them I was stranded in Billings."

He wanted to hug her, which might have led to something embarrassing, like him blushing, but like she'd done many times, Minnie saved him from himself. "You boys need to get cleaned up before you sit on my furniture. Go on, shoo."

Thalia barely hid her giggle behind her hand before she pushed him toward the stairs. "She's right, you know," she called out behind them.

"That seemed to go well," Hoss said as they took the stairs.

J.R. knew he should not engage, should *not* run the risk of provoking Hoss's smart mouth, but he couldn't help himself. The man was more than his best friend, he was his brother. "You think?"

"Yup." They reached the top of the stairs, and Hoss turned to look at him. "It's odd, you know."

J.R. swallowed, refusing to be nervous as his friend passed judgment on this thing with Thalia. "What is?"

"Seeing you smile." Hoss was completely, totally serious, with nary a wisecrack in sight. The sentiment was so real, so unexpected, J.R. didn't know what to do.

The moment didn't last. "I forgot you had so many teeth." Hoss threw his hands up in front of his eyes and staggered back. "Damn, man. Put those things away before you blind me." Chuckling, he didn't even wait for whatever snappy comeback J.R. didn't have. He headed down to his room, peeling off layers as he went.

J.R. took his time getting cleaned up. Thalia's bag sat on the end of his bed, the promise of another night in her arms making him want to rush. However, rushing was the last thing he wanted to do. He spent a few extra minutes taking his beard down a layer and cleaning up the edges. His first instinct was to shave the whole thing off—he'd never had a beard and a lady friend at the same time—but something told him that was the wrong move, and that something was the memory of all the little noises Thalia made in the dark.

Down, boy, he thought as he wrangled his button fly. He

still had to make it through dinner, and it would probably be bad form to throw Thalia over his shoulder and carry her away the moment the plates were in the dishwasher. Which meant he had to keep his cool for another couple of hours. He could do that.

He hoped.

It turned out the time moved at a comfortable pace. Thalia and Minnie had, if possible, become even better friends over the course of the afternoon, and were now talking about movie stars who did TV shows. That wasn't so unusual, he guessed, but the way they kept drawing him, and even Hoss, into the conversation was, well, odd. It should have felt like he was being cornered for all his insider info—after all, he had known several of the actors they were talking about—but no one plumbed him for dirt, or expected him to have the right answer. Thalia asked him what he thought, he stated his piece and they talked about it. If anything, she had way more insider info than he did. All of his knowledge was sorely out of date.

After dinner was over, Minnie said, "J.R., why don't you show Thalia the rest of the house? She's going to think we live in the kitchen."

"What about me?" Hoss asked. He had the nerve to look hopeful. J.R. wanted to smack that puppy-dog face right off him.

"You can help with the dishes," Minnie replied in her no-nonsense tone before she motioned for J.R. to go on.

"Come on," J.R. said, taking Thalia's hand as he led her into the hallway that divided the house in two. They left a winking Minnie and a grumbling Hoss in the kitchen. "This is the dining room."

She took in the table built to seat fourteen. "My, what a big table you have."

He couldn't help but grin at her. "We only use it during the summer, when we've got hired hands to feed."

"That's a lot of hired help." She was impressed, he could tell.

"I've got about six guys who stay the whole summer out in the bunkhouse, and some other local fellows who come out for the day. I pay them, but I think they stay for Minnie's cooking." He leaned down, getting close enough to her that he could smell the scent of strawberries. "More than one of the older guys has proposed to her, you know."

Thalia gave him a sly smile. "The way to a cowboy's heart is his stomach?" Then she leaned up on her tiptoes and placed an innocent-feeling kiss on his lips.

Yeah, the stomach was one way—but not the only one. He tried to pull her in closer, but she pushed back on his chest and shot him a look that managed to walk the line between scolding and teasing. "You're supposed to be showing me around."

"And you're supposed to be looking." Man, he liked that smile on her. He liked being the one who brought it out even more. Somewhat begrudgingly, he moved her across the entry hallway. He didn't let go of her waist this time. He wanted to keep a hold of her as much as he could.

He led her past the front stairs and into the open room on the other side of the house. "This is the living room." She shot him a sideways glance, as if she didn't believe him. "Well, it is." The massive TV took up the wall opposite of the hearth. A pool table was in one corner, and Minnie had leather armchairs everywhere. The architect had wanted to make this two separate rooms—a parlor, he'd said, and a family room. J.R. had nixed that idea straight out. At the time, he'd assumed he'd never have a family. And the kitchen did double duty, anyway.

Thalia leaned back into him, rubbing her hand over his beard before snaking it up into his hair and pulling his head down to her neck. "I see. You use this more in the summer, too?" It was a perfectly polite question, but the way she shimmied her hips against his button fly was anything but polite. In fact, it bordered on cruel.

"Yeah," was all he got out as he scraped his facial hair over her earlobe. *That's right,* he thought, *two could play at this game.*

With great reluctance, she released him. "What's through there?"

Hell, yes, he was excited to hear how much of an impact he was having on her—her voice was strained. "The office."

Moving slowly, they maneuvered their way around all the chairs and through the doorway, all without taking their hands off each other. J.R. couldn't remember feeling this hot for a woman, and he couldn't remember a time when a woman had seemed this hot for him. James Robert, sure. Lots of women wanted to sleep with him for the record books. Even his few nights with lady friends since then hadn't had this urgency, this *need* behind them.

He spun her around and backed her up against his desk. Or maybe it was Hoss's desk—hell, he didn't know. It was a desk, and she was against it. Against him.

The full weight of her breasts pressed against him, high and heavy and begging for him to touch, so he did. He cupped them both, feeling her nipples peaking through all of her clothes beneath his thumbs. "J.R." His name came out as a low moan, like it had last night. She tilted her hips up, brushing her center against the front of his jeans as she dragged his mouth to hers.

Whoa. The kiss was one of those no-holds-barred kinds that obliterated anything else but *this* woman. He was straining so hard behind his fly that he was in danger of breaking his jeans. The ache ran deeper than that, though—it went all the way through him. She made him *hurt* in the best possible way. She was his pain and his salvation at the same time.

He was in over his head. Luckily, his head wasn't wasting too much time thinking about that. "Yeah. This is the office."

"Nice," she agreed, sliding her hands down his waist and over his backside.

What little control he had left—and he was damnably impressed he had any—helped him to realize that sex in the office would be crossing a line that even Minnie wouldn't let slide. "That's the downstairs."

Her eyes shined in a co-conspiratorial way. "I haven't seen everything upstairs. Haven't seen your room. Minnie moved my things," she added before he could ask.

"I should show you." It was almost impossible to let go of her enough that they could get the hell out of this room, but he forced himself to take a step back.

She was better at this than he was. He could tell because, even though she pushed him back, her chest was heaving and her eyes blazed with the same kind of barely contained desire that held a tight grip on him.

"Front," was all he could say, but she understood. No need to cut through the kitchen and get bogged down in chitchat with Minnie about how well Thalia liked the house. A distraction like that would kill him.

With long strides, she almost pulled him to the front stairway. He let her go up in front of him for selfish reasons—so he could watch her bottom move at eye level. As much as he was trying to be a mature, responsible lover, he couldn't resist skimming his hands over the back of her jeans. She giggled, which he took as a good sign.

All the way down the hall, he touched her. He squeezed her bottom, ran his hands over her hips, slipped his fingertips below her waistband. Anything to get closer to the skin he'd barely gotten to touch last night. Anything to get closer to her.

They ran into his door with a thud. He was still behind her, and he took this moment to slip his hand down the front of her jeans. One hand on her warm center, the other stroking her breast, his mouth on her neck, her ear—if he didn't need to get rid of all these clothes, he'd hold her here and make her come.

When she said, *"Please,"* in a low, whimpering voice, he knew he couldn't wait. He needed her too much.

He fumbled the doorknob open, and they all but fell into his room. It wasn't warm—the fire was far too low in the hearth to add much heat to the room—but it wasn't as cold as last night had been. He managed to kick the door shut at the same time he grabbed the hem of her sweater and peeled it over her head.

Disappointment came in the form of a white tank top. But the black straps of her bra peeked out at her shoulders, so that kept him going. He lifted the top over her head and was immediately rewarded with the full view of her breasts, barely contained by the black lace.

"Wow," he said, unable to keep his hands to himself. He let their luscious weight fill his hands again.

Another low moan escaped her lips. He covered her mouth with his, feeling the sound of her pleasure rocket through him. Then they were moving again. He was pushing her back toward the bed, she was working each agonizing button on his fly, and he was trying to undo her bra strap. He was out of practice. Took three times to get the whole thing undone.

They hit the bed, a tangle of arms and legs and clothing flying off every which way. Man, how he wanted to slow down and appreciate her body, to let her know how special she was, how she made him feel—but he couldn't. It wasn't physically possible to take it nice and easy with her pushing his jeans and his boxers down, with her wrapping her long fingers around his shaft, with her arching her back as he sucked on her breast. Hell, it wasn't even possible to get all the way *on* the bed. He couldn't wait. He had to have her right now.

With one foot tangled in his jeans and still on the floor, he lifted her legs until she had them wrapped around his waist.

"Yes," she hissed, running her fingers over his chest hair as he positioned himself. Then, with two hard thrusts, he was lodged deep in her welcoming body, feeling her shiver and shake as she cried out.

Oh, yeah, he thought, but he didn't have the voice to say it. Her body was tight and wet around him as he drove into her. Her hands moved over him without rhyme or reason— stroking his face, rubbing over his nipples, running her nails down his back with enough pressure to make him groan. It was the only noise he was capable of making.

"Yes, *yes,*" she kept saying, and he knew he was doing that to her, for her. He was the one she wanted—not James Robert, not Hoss—not anyone. Just him. When she said, "J.R.!" as she grabbed hold of his hip bones and pulled him even deeper into her, well, he lost it. He couldn't control himself.

With a final thrust, he came as her shock waves rolled through her. The feeling was so *much* that he lost his balance and fell on top of her with a muffled *whump*. He was worried he'd hurt her, but she giggled again and wrapped her arms around him.

She held him. It shouldn't have felt like a big deal— especially not compared with the amazing sex—but it was, and J.R. wasn't sure why. She hugged him tight to her chest. He felt her heartbeat steady and her chest rise and fall more regularly.

He managed to prop himself up on one arm. He didn't want to crush her, after all. This would be the time to come up with some smooth line, some tender pillow talk—all things he'd done in the past and was perfectly capable of doing again.

But when he looked into her eyes, he had nothing— nothing except the feeling of being both lost and found at the same time. He was lost—to her.

She smiled, a small, special thing that made him ache again. "So," she said, her voice still smiling for her. "This is the bedroom."

"Yup." *Keep it together,* he yelled at himself. He managed to pat the bed next to her head. "This is the bed."

"Nice." She leaned up and kissed him—not the fevered thing from before, but a touch of honesty.

He pulled out and managed to get back on his feet. He wasn't as young as he once was, back when a wild night of drunken partying was a standard Saturday, but he hoped he had enough gas in the tank to make one more go of it tonight. Later, he promised himself, he'd take his time. "Be right back."

He got cleaned up in a hurry. When he got back to the bedroom, she had a sheet wrapped around her. "Cold?"

"A little." She grinned at him in all his naked glory, which was basically cheating. He needed this room to be a lot warmer so she wouldn't hide behind a sheet.

"I'll get the fire going." When the bathroom door shut, he slipped his boxers back on and got to work on the fire. By the time she came out a few minutes later, he'd built a respectable blaze.

Still wrapped in that damn sheet, she came up next to him and rested her head against his arm. Wrapping her up in a hug, he pulled her in close. They stood like that for a few minutes. He knew she was looking at his Oscar and all the photos on the wall, but it didn't feel like a dangerous act, not like it had with Donna.

"Do you miss him?"

Thalia's question caught him off guard. "Who?" he asked, trying to figure out which of the celebrities in the photos she was referring to. All of them had been professional acquaintances, at best.

"Him." She stepped forward and touched a photo of James Robert posing with a young Brad Pitt. J.R knew he'd been about twenty in that photo. It felt like a lifetime ago.

She wasn't touching Brad's face in the photo.

"Do you ever miss being James Robert?"

J.R. felt himself breathe. She didn't ask like she couldn't believe he'd given up all that fame and money. She didn't weigh down her words with expectations of what he should be, should do. She just asked—and waited for the answer.

If it had been anyone else, he'd have gone on the defensive, loudly protesting how much he'd hated that life, how much he loved this new one he'd made for himself. But he didn't have to lie to her. He didn't have to lie to himself anymore.

"Sometimes. I get up at 3:30 a.m. in the summer to work cattle. I get stepped on, kicked, crapped on—you name it. Everyone has bad days, and when I have a bad day, it's my own damn fault, and no one else is going to come along and clean up my mess." Like the mess he'd made in Denny's bar the other night. J.R. had screwed up, and he had to deal with the consequences. "And I do miss the warm weather some days."

She shot him a silly smile. "And to think—I'm enjoying my first blizzard."

"Anytime you want to come back out here and be snowed in, you let me know." It was supposed to sound flippant, supposed to be this funny little joke he told, but it didn't come out that way. Not even close. All he heard himself say was, *Come back to me.* He didn't want this feeling, this, well, happiness to end when the snow melted. Honestly, he didn't think he wanted it to end at all.

The silliness of her grin faded a little bit, and she looked sad. He wasn't sure why, and he was afraid to find out. Maybe she didn't feel the same way about him? Then she said, "That goes for you, too. Anytime you want to hit a beach, you come see me. Just you," she added, curling into his arms. "No movie stars allowed."

Oh, yeah. He was lost to her, but it was okay.

She'd found him.

Thirteen

The next five days were some of the best ones J.R. could remember. He woke up with Thalia's arms around him. They made sweet love in the morning and then, after breakfast, bundled up and went out to the barn together. He even saddled up Old Coot and let her walk him around the arena. The way her face almost cracked in two from her smile was more than enough reward.

After that, he'd take her back into the house, pick up Hoss and do his best to get hay out to his herds. He'd come home to happy women and a hot meal. A couple of nights after dinner, they lit the fire in the living room and watched a movie while eating popcorn. Then back to bed, back to her arms. Back to loving on her.

Thalia shouldn't have fit in his house—his life—so well, but she did. Minnie was thrilled to have someone to talk to and help out with the meals. Hoss settled into a nice place of gentle teasing without being over the top, and J.R. was, well…

He was in danger of falling for Thalia.

That was a problem because, sooner or later, the snow would melt, and she'd go back to Hollywood and he'd still be out here. And that would take everything easy about being with Thalia and make the rest of his life hard to swallow.

She was the best thing to ever happen to him. How the hell was he going to let her drive away?

He tried not to think about it, reasoning the snow would keep her out here.

Except it didn't. On the fifth day after the blizzard, the temperatures spiked up to thirty-nine, which didn't make much of a dent in the depth of the snow. The next day, it was forty-four, and the day after that, it hit fifty-two. Fifty-two damn degrees on January 29. In Montana.

Hoss kept plowing the drive, making more progress every day. J.R. entertained notions of sabotaging the bulldozer, but he knew that would come back to bite him on the butt, so he didn't. On the third straight day of mid-fifties weather, Hoss made it to the road.

"It's clear enough," he reported at dinner, his eyebrows notched in worry. "Road's probably good to Billings."

"I don't know if I can drive that far on clear enough," Thalia said. "I haven't driven on snow in a long time."

"J.R. will take you, and we'll get the rental back to Billings for you," Minnie offered in what was supposed to be a helpful tone. It made J.R. want to yell at her. What were the two of them trying to do, push Thalia out of here?

"You can stay as long as you want." He told her that at dinner, and he told her that in bed that night, the scent of sex still hanging over them. He wanted to tell her she could stay forever, but it sounded crazy, even to him.

"I have to get back." He hugged her tight, wishing she wasn't right but knowing she was. "But not tomorrow."

"Yeah. One more day," he said. One more day of happiness.

How was he going to let her go?

There had to be a way. He just didn't know what it was.

That last day together was hard on Thalia. She knew she needed to be enjoying every last second of her time with J.R., but reality was too insistent. She was heading home tomorrow morning—where she'd have to face Levinson without the actor she'd promised to deliver. She had no doubt he'd fire her on the spot, and she had little doubt he'd make sure she didn't get another job.

Inevitable unemployment wasn't what she found the most depressing. No, the most depressing thing was that she was going to have to say goodbye to J.R. True, they'd get a few extra hours together on the drive to Billings, but then she'd get on her plane and he'd get back in his truck, and that would be that.

Maybe not, she found herself hoping. He'd said she could come back; she'd invited him out to California. Maybe she'd see him again. Maybe this wasn't *The End*. Maybe it was *To Be Continued*...

Of course, the last time she'd attempted a long-distance relationship had been when she left her college boyfriend behind to go to Hollywood in the first place, and that hadn't made it a month before the relationship fell to bits.

The whole thing sucked. She couldn't give up the life she had—the career she'd made—to take up with a rancher, even if that rancher was J.R. This wasn't the movies, after all. This was real life.

So, on February 2, she packed up her things and carried her bags down to the kitchen. J.R. was outside with Hoss, which was just as well. He'd been quiet the whole night and morning, and Thalia wanted to say goodbye to Minnie without any men around. She was pretty sure there would be tears.

"You'll let me know how it goes?" Minnie said while hugging Thalia.

"Of course." How could she not let Minnie know how the firing went? "You'll take care of J.R. for me, won't you?"

"Oh," Minnie said, sniffling a little as she waved the question away. "I predict a few months of temper tantrums after this." Thalia guessed it was supposed to be a little joke, but it almost broke her heart.

J.R. and Hoss came back in, and J.R. went upstairs to get his bag. He'd told Thalia he was packing a change of clothes, in case the roads were bad enough that he couldn't make it home in the dark. That left Thalia with a sniffling Minnie and Hoss, who looked as uncomfortable as a man of his size could. "Thalia," he said, sticking out a hand for what was bound to be an awkward handshake.

"Hoss." She couldn't leave it at a shake. These people had become too important to her. She gave him one of those awkward hugs with their clasped hands in between their bodies.

"Don't forget, I'm still looking for a casting couch."

"I'll do my darnedest to find you a good one." Thalia had to blink a couple of times to keep the tears from spilling over.

Then she heard J.R. thumping back down the stairs. Putting on the happiest face she could muster, she turned to him.

He stood there, taking in the scene. He had a duffel bag in his hand, a hat on his head—and a suiter slung over his shoulder. "J.R.?"

He locked his gaze on her. "I'm going with you."

She couldn't tell if this was a dream come true—he wanted to come with her—or a nightmare of epic proportions. "What? No—you can't!"

A look crossed his face—the same look he'd given her on that first day, when he'd left her out in the cold. It sent a chill through her. "I'm not saying I'll take the part. But I'll meet with Levinson."

"But—but—but you hate him! And if word gets out about you, the press will come after you—you have no idea what it's like these days, J.R.!" The irony of her words struck her.

Was she actively trying to keep him from coming with her? Really?

"I'm not afraid of him or anyone." He squared his shoulders. "I can take it. I'm coming with you."

He was doing this for her. She knew that with unwavering certainty. He wasn't protecting himself. He wasn't throwing her under the bus—or, as he said it, in front of the bus. He was putting himself at risk for *her*.

No one had ever laid it on the line for her before. He'd said it himself—a real man made sure a lady was safe. If he came, if he took the part, if he made a big return to the screen, she'd get to keep her job. She might even get to see him on a semiregular basis, especially while they were filming. It could work.

But he wouldn't be happy being famous again. She knew it—and so did he.

"No."

That was the hell of it. He wanted to come with her, she wanted him to come with her—but she had to protect him. From himself, it seemed. She couldn't let him throw away everything he'd worked for, just for her.

The tension in the room felt like a rubber band about to snap. J.R. leveled those beautiful amber eyes at her. God, he would be her undoing. "I'm coming with you, and that's final."

"I'll make Hoss take me."

This threat proved empty before the words had dissipated out of the air. Hoss coughed behind her. "Sorry, Thalia. I got work to do."

The desperation that gripped Thalia was sadly familiar. She wasn't going to be able to talk herself out of this. She couldn't control the situation—instead, the situation was controlling her. Still, she heard herself say, "Minnie?"

"I don't drive on snow if I can help it," Minnie said, her voice small. "Black ice," she added.

One corner of J.R.'s mouth curled up, a smile in victory. He looked like a mercenary. "I'm going."

"It'll change everything."

That wasn't some half-baked attempt to stall. That was the truth. Everything would be different for him. For her, too.

His face softened. He looked less deadly, more thoughtful. "Maybe it should." Then he picked up her bag and walked out the door.

"Take care of him," Minnie said, and Thalia heard the catch in her voice.

"I will." It felt like an empty promise, though. Taking care of him would be making sure his secret was safe—that he was safe. Letting him come to Hollywood? How was she supposed to take care of him there?

The path Hoss had plowed was passable, at best, and she was extra glad she didn't have to drive. J.R. was silent, both hands gripping the wheel. She wanted to try and talk him out of making the journey with her, but she also didn't want to make him drive into a snowbank.

Hoss had been right—the road was pretty good, once they reached it. J.R. loosened his grip on the wheel and relaxed back into his seat a little. They still had a long way to go, though.

Again, she found herself knowing she had to plead her case to J.R. and not knowing how to go about it. At least this time, she wasn't in danger of freezing to death.

She'd spent a week and a half in this man's bed. Trying to talk to him shouldn't seem like such a treacherous mountain to climb.

"Listen," she started, because she didn't have any better ideas but also because that's what she wanted him to do.

"No, I understand how it is. Beautiful, intelligent woman like you—you probably have someone else."

He thought she'd lied to him. "That's what you think?"

His only response was a curt nod of his head.

"J.R., you listen to me. The only thing I want more than for you to come with me is for me to stay with you. But I can't—and not because I've got some other lover stashed somewhere. The only reason I'm trying—*trying*—to talk you out of getting on that plane with me is because I know it won't work."

"It could," was his gruff reply.

"It won't—and not because we don't want it to. It won't work because sooner or later, you'll be James Robert Bradley again, and the moment that happens, the *moment* you lose J.R., you'll hate it all over again. And since I'm the reason you gave it up, you'll…" *Hate me.* She couldn't say the words. She hated having to say these things, hated having to break her own heart. Most of all, she hated being right.

Because she was. When she'd shown up on his porch that first day, she hadn't cared about J.R. All she had cared about was the great press James Robert Bradley would bring to the role, the tickets his comeback performance would sell.

All that had changed. Now, money was the last thing on her mind. The man was more important. The man, she realized, was everything.

Unable to keep her tears back, she turned to look out the passenger side window. It was better this way, she tried to tell herself. Better to end it now, when they could just be unhappy with each other, before both of their lives got turned upside down and inside out. She'd seen that happen too many times. People on a set—away from their real lives—fell madly in love, only to watch the whole thing disintegrate on them when they had to go back to the real world.

She didn't want that to happen to them.

The silence in the cab of the truck weighed down on her. *Breathe,* she told herself.

J.R. cleared his throat. Thalia tensed, but he didn't say anything for a few more agonizing seconds. "You aren't seeing anyone else?"

"No. Dating within the industry is a death trap on the best

of days." Why did she have to defend herself here? She'd been
honest with him. She hadn't slept with anyone in a year. She'd
dumped her last boyfriend before Valentine's Day as a matter of self-preservation.

Of course, the moment she thought that, guilt rushed in.
She hadn't been completely honest. She hadn't told him about
her disastrous affair with Levinson. When she'd been leaving
and he'd been staying, it hadn't seemed relevant. But now?

The silence stretched for another painful minute. Thalia
couldn't decide if she should keep her mouth shut or tell J.R.
about her messy history with Levinson.

Was it any of his business who she had or had not slept
with in the past? They were lovers now—obviously. That
didn't necessarily entitle her to the list—and she knew it was
long—of his previous paramours, both of the famous and not-
so-famous variety. Why would it be any different for him?

The past was just that—the past, she decided.

"I'm, uh, not real good with apologizing." J.R.'s hesitant
statement should have been awkward, but instead it only
made Thalia want to smile. She looked at him. His eyes were
still glued to the road, but his face had relaxed. He was in
danger of smiling.

No, he wasn't good at apologies. But he was willing to attempt it. For her. "Practice makes perfect."

He reached over and squeezed her leg. Then they hit a slick
spot and he had to put both hands back on the wheel. "Look,
I know it's going to be hard. But you're…" He cleared his
throat again. Thalia felt like she should look away from him,
so he could get what he was about to say off his chest. He was
incapable of talking with eye contact. At least, out of bed.

So she moved her gaze to the windshield and waited.

"You're important to me and I'll fight to be with you."
The words came out in a rush, like air escaping a balloon.

Now how was she supposed to argue with that? Was she
supposed to say that she wasn't that important? Tell him he

didn't mean as much to her as she did to him? Was she supposed to lie to his face and tell him that wasn't one of the more romantic things anyone had ever said to her? That he didn't make her melt?

No. There wasn't any way to argue with the fact that she was important to him, and he was willing to take a huge risk for her.

"It's my choice. Even if it isn't the best one, I want to be the one who makes it. And I choose to hold on to you right now. If you don't feel the same way, I'll understand." This time, he didn't talk like he was mad at the world. His voice was tender again, more questioning than demanding.

Thalia couldn't remember if she was supposed to breathe in or out and wound up coughing. "You okay?" he asked, giving her leg another quick squeeze.

Nothing ventured, nothing gained. Things could still go a thousand ways wrong, but she had to take a chance—*this* chance—that things would go right. She had to trust him, and she had to trust herself.

She leaned over and touched his cheek. "I don't think I've ever been better, J.R."

Fourteen

One thing was for sure. J.R. wasn't used to traveling anymore. The drive to Billings wasn't so bad, but the puddle jumper to Denver about did him in, and the 737 to LAX wasn't much better. Even from first class.

Another thing he learned real quick was that, even though he could handle a Montana summer, he wasn't ready for the warm air that hit him in the face the moment they stepped outside the airport in sunny California. Despite having to deal with manure on a daily basis, the smell of L.A. made his head hurt. Was that a new odor, or had he just not noticed it before?

The throng of people was the third thing that set him back on his heels. Yeah, he had a lot of cowboys on the ranch in the summer, and yeah, he did fine in the bar in Beaverhead, even when it was crowded.

But he'd forgotten about the sheer volume of humanity that walked around L.A., often in outfits that barely qualified as clothing. Thalia had offered to put him up at the Chateau Marmont, but he had too many memories of the hotel where

Hollywood went to party. When she had then suggested he stay at her place, he jumped all over it. After all, it didn't matter so much about the noise or the people or the smell as long as he was with her. It felt strange to sleep in a different bed, but she was in it with him, so it wasn't that strange at all.

The next day, instead of hiding from people who might or might not recognize him, he'd spent part of the afternoon sitting in a coffee shop a block away from Thalia's apartment, reading *Variety* and drinking cups of coffee with six-word names while she was at work. He'd watched the people, too. Everyone was so skinny here, with the women all looking eerily similar to plastic dolls and the men appearing to be waxed within an inch of their lives. J.R. had found himself stroking his chin. Very few beards around here. He stuck out like a sore thumb, which didn't jibe well with the whole trying-to-be-invisible angle he was working on.

Thalia had called a couple of hours ago, after she got out of her meeting with Levinson. Yes, he was excited to hear J.R. was interested in the part, but he didn't want to wait until tomorrow, she'd said. There was a party happening tonight at some club that hadn't existed eleven years ago. If she'd told him what the party was for, he didn't remember. Everything but the fact that he was going to have to go to a social event with God only knew how many celebrities—and accompanying paparazzi—washed over him.

"You don't have to go," Thalia had said when he hadn't come back with a response.

On the one hand, he liked that she wanted to protect him. He knew his trust in her wasn't misplaced, that she cared for him. It made him want to spend another night making love to her—to hell with parties.

On the other hand, it was a direct blow to his male pride. He would not cower in this apartment, by God. He *didn't* cower. "It's fine."

The pause had been long, and he could see her trying to

decide if she should argue with him or let it ride. "I'll be home in an hour. We'll eat dinner and go. We won't stay long, not if you don't want to."

"It's fine," was all he had been capable of saying.

Which is how he found himself standing in Thalia's bathroom, wearing nothing but a towel and a beard. The options weighed heavy on him.

No one else in this town seemed to have a beard, not a full one like his. It wasn't like he was married to the beard. He shaved in the summer, when extra insulation wasn't required. Plus, he cleaned up well. If he shaved, he'd look more like his old self, the celebrity people would recognize.

But he didn't want to be what people expected, not anymore. He lived his life on his terms now. Maybe he should keep it. Thalia loved it, after all. It'd be a quick 'n' easy way to announce to these people that he didn't play by their rules. He didn't have to conform to their expectations. He was his own man, for crying out loud, and he could wear a beard if he wanted.

Jeez, it was like the beard was his life. Did he want to look like James Robert or J.R.?

Who the hell was he?

"Screw it," he muttered to himself. Ten minutes later, he rinsed off his face and looked at his reflection. God, he hoped Thalia liked it.

He'd never worn a goatee, but sometimes, a man had to split the difference.

"Ms. Thorne," a beefy, bald bouncer said, nodding his head in greeting. He lifted the velvet rope—they still had velvet ropes, so that hadn't changed—and motioned her up the staircase in the middle of the club. The thing seemed to be made of solid glass, and J.R. saw a go-go dancer, or whatever they were called now, gyrating on the landing halfway up.

Thalia led the way, which gave J.R. a chance to appreciate the fine view of her backside in a skintight red cocktail dress that was backless. As far as he could tell, the dress didn't make any allowances for underthings of any sort, and his imagination was running rampant. Raw desire was the only thing that kept him from panicking at this point.

The club pulsed with a bass beat timed to strobe lights. Men and women made out with women and men everywhere, which was unnerving enough, but plenty of them were breaking their embraces to stare at him. Once, this had been his life. Hit a club, get smashed, pick up a chick, have forgettable sex. He looked back at the people staring at him. Once, he'd been one of them. Not anymore.

"Whoa, cowboy. Name?" The beefy bouncer held him back with a hand on his chest. Already on edge, it took a lot of work to keep from snapping the man's fingers.

"He's on the list, Trevor." Thalia turned back and scrolled down the man's tablet—clipboards had gone out of fashion, apparently. "There. Bradley."

At least the bouncer uniform hadn't changed much—black pants, black T-shirt. Trevor gave J.R. the once-over, clearly amused by the crocodile-skin boots, the Stetson and the bolo tie. "Enjoy the party, Mr. Bradley."

Fat chance that would happen, but Thalia gave him an encouraging smile before she began to climb the stairs again.

He wished he could hold her hand, but even he had seen the folly of public displays of affection in front of Levinson and associates. For all intents and purposes, he and Thalia were business acquaintances and nothing more.

That became a problem, at least for him, as they reached the private party on the second floor. Women—and men— greeted Thalia with kisses on the cheeks, and J.R. felt himself getting the kind of jealous that only led to trouble. He knew the rituals but it still bugged him to watch other men touch her. She was his, as much as he was hers.

It got worse. Everyone knew he was here, but no one knew

who he was. He swore he heard whispers over the grinding music. Maybe he should have worn all black and shaved the beard. He wouldn't have looked like himself, but he would have been almost invisible here.

"Who's this tall drink of water?" a woman J.R. didn't recognize said. She was all but licking her chops as her gaze swept over him like a hungry cat.

"Kathryn, this is James Robert Bradley."

J.R. knew she was going to do that—they'd game-planned out how to handle the party and the people. But it still felt almost like a physical blow below the solar plexus. Damn near knocked the wind out of him.

"*The* James Robert Bradley?"

That was part of the script he and Thalia had discussed. At this point, he was loving the script. "One and the same, ma'am." And he tipped his hat, mostly to keep her from kissing him.

Kathryn whoever's hand flew to her mouth. "Oh, my God, *the* James Robert Bradley? I thought you were dead!"

"Nope. Just ranching." He wasn't going to mention the state. Thalia had agreed that the less identifying information he gave out, the better everything would be.

"You," this Kathryn said, her eyes narrowing as a manicured nail flicked in his direction, "were supposed to give me my Oscar, and you bailed. They had to get Tom to give it to me. I've never forgiven you for that."

Oh, hell. He should know who this Kathryn was. Luckily, Thalia came to his rescue. "Excuse us, I see Bob," she said with a gracious smile before she took him by the elbow and led him away. "Great job," she added in a low voice. "Only another two hundred to go."

He tried to laugh, but it got stuck in his throat. "I could go for a beer right now."

"They might have one at the bar." She angled him in a different direction.

"Might?" He glanced around. Everyone else had martini glasses with fruity drinks. No one was drinking a simple beer. Man, he was out of his league here.

Getting to the bar took some time. Word of his continual living spread like wildfire and a crowd started to form. Young guys started telling him how he had been such an inspiration, older women looked at him like hungry dogs staring at a bone, and a few men—men he'd known and partied with—slapped him on the back and told him he had on "a hell of a hat for Hollywood."

"Where *have* you been?" That question came from Eli Granger, who J.R. remembered as a young punk actor bent on self-destruction but now, according to Thalia, was a respectable agent.

"Not here."

Eli snorted as he sipped his Cristal. "Was 'not here' good, man?"

"'Not here' was great," he admitted, casting a glance at Thalia. He couldn't tell in this crappy light, but she might have blushed. J.R. wondered how far down that blush went if she didn't have on anything underneath the dress.

Eli slapped him on the back. "I'm almost jealous." His self-confident mask fell away, and J.R. saw a guy who was tired of running a race he was never going to win. J.R. recognized that look. He'd been tired once. It had almost killed him.

"You should come visit 'not here' sometime. It's normal there, if you like cows." He couldn't believe he was extending the offer to a man who was more or less a complete stranger, but once, he and Eli had been whatever passed as friends in this place.

"Thanks, but I don't eat red meat." As quick as his mask had fallen off, Eli was back to sipping his expensive champagne and looking cynical.

And so it went. Thalia got J.R. some brand of beer he'd never heard of from the bar, but hey, it was a beer and he drank it. Slowly. The four-beer limit was in effect here, too. She stayed close to him, guiding introductions and extracting him from conversations that started to spiral out of control, which happened a lot. Half the people in the room were either drunk or high. Or both.

J.R. was able to relax enough to appreciate her skills. She knew every single person by name and had a compliment at the ready at all times without giving anything away. She flattered egos and said the right thing about projects finished or coming soon. She was good at what she did, he saw. A realization that was followed by a tinge of disappointment. She fit well here. She wouldn't want to give this up to come live with an occasionally cranky rancher in the middle of nowhere.

He shoved those thoughts aside and focused on surviving the evening. After what felt like several hours of meeting and greeting, they made their way back to where Bob Levinson was holding court.

He was shorter than J.R. remembered, with a barrel chest contained by a three-piece suit. Once, J.R. remembered Levinson had been passably handsome. No more. One too many face-lifts or Botox or whatever people did to themselves here had left Levinson looking like a clownish version of himself. His hair hadn't changed, though—shoe-polish black and slicked into an embarrassment of a ponytail. A watch chain hung out of his vest pocket, and his cuff links appeared to be gemstones. As if he needed further accessorizing, he sat in a booth with four different women wearing blond hair and spandex dresses. He looked like a pimp for the mutual fund set.

Thalia started to introduce J.R., but Levinson cut her off. "Well, well. Look who's back." Levinson's voice hadn't aged well. He'd always had a weak spot for cigars and cocaine, which meant he both sounded and smelled old.

"Bob," Thalia said, apparently determined to press on. "You remember James."

The ladies around Levinson shifted as they appraised him. He didn't tip his hat, but he nodded in greeting. One of them waggled her fingers at him.

Levinson sat there, looking at him with a greedy little smile on his face. J.R. knew that look. That was the look that said J.R. wasn't a man standing here. He was a commodity to be bought and sold.

Damn, but he hated that feeling.

"Ladies." Levinson shooed them all out of the booth, then he looked at Thalia. "You, too."

J.R. looked at Thalia, who was about to crack that smile right off her face. She didn't like this; he didn't like it. But Levinson was the one calling the shots. "I'll get you another beer," she said before she stiffly turned and walked away.

This wasn't part of the script.

"Sit down." Levinson clearly hadn't gotten any more into the habit of social graces in the interim.

"I'll stand." That was the nice thing about not caring about the part or his career or what anyone else—besides Thalia—thought of him. He could do whatever he wanted, and more than anything, he didn't want to take orders from this slimy man.

Levinson's oily smile faded a little. He looked like a barracuda ready to strike. "Damn shame about your mother. She was a wonderful woman."

They both knew that was a bald-faced lie. J.R. knew he hadn't forgotten what condescending compliments were like, but he hadn't exactly remembered how freaking irritating it was. "You let me know when you're done with the B.S."

Levinson didn't miss a beat. "This is going to be a big winner, James. Another Oscar for your collection." He looked J.R. up and down with a calculating eye. "Hell, think of the money we'll save on wardrobe alone." He leaned forward and snorted a line of coke off the tabletop.

Ugh, J.R. thought. Once upon a time, he might have done

the same to feel like he belonged. Not anymore. He stood his ground, waiting for the B.S. to be over.

It wasn't. "She's something, isn't she?" The way he said it set the hackles up on J.R.'s neck.

"Who?" He knew who, but he was praying that Levinson was talking about one of the bimbos.

Levinson leaned back, clearly lost in the rush of his high. "She said she'd find you, and she said she'd bring you back— signed, sealed and delivered. What did it take?" He grinned, an ugly, leering thing that seemed three sizes too big for his small head. "Did she make it worth your while?"

The suggestion was anything but subtle. J.R. felt his temper beginning to flare, but he fought to keep it cool. "I don't know what you're talking about." Except he did. Once, he'd accused Thalia of doing just that, and she'd properly slapped him for it. Now that he knew her, he knew she wouldn't use sex to trap him.

"Oh, she's amazing." Even though J.R. could tell by the look on Levinson's face that he was intentionally trying to get a reaction out of him, it was still working. It was all J.R. could do to keep his fist clenched as Levinson went on, "Damn shame her acting career died on the vine. She had potential. Of course, after my wife found out about us, well…" He shrugged, looking anything but apologetic. "You know Miranda and her unique talent to make things difficult."

Something in J.R.'s brain misfired, so he tried to turn his mental engine over what Levinson had said a second time. Had he said that he and Thalia had been an "us"? Had she seriously had an affair with this *slimebag?* Why hadn't Thalia told him—at least to warn him? They'd scripted out the entire evening—and she hadn't bothered to mention this as a conversational death trap? And if she hadn't told him something important, like the fact that she'd been intimate with this—this—*man,* what else wasn't she telling him? What else was a lie?

"How is your wife?" This last gasp at civility was all he had to hold on to before he broke something. Or someone.

Levinson waved off the comment. "Left me for a younger man. Good riddance." His eyes narrowed as he wiped a thin trail of cocaine-snot off his nose. "Or did you not have her? She told me she'd do whatever it took to get you here, and," he said, sweeping his hands across the booth, "here you are."

If J.R. were in Montana instead of California, he'd have already broken Levinson's nose. And maybe a few other bones. "I haven't signed anything yet." Then, because he was losing the last of his self-control, he added, "I was waiting to see if I could stomach working with you again. You couldn't pay me enough money in the world to have another conversation with you, much less do a movie. You can take your Oscars and shove them where the sun don't shine."

Three things happened in quick succession. One, a hush fell over the club. Even the DJ paused the pounding beat, and J.R. got the sense that everyone—*everyone*—was listening to him do the unprecedented and say *no* to Bob Levinson. The second thing was that anything jovial or, heaven forbid, cheerful about Levinson stopped cold, and J.R. found himself looking at an ugly old man.

The third thing was that Thalia chose that moment to reenter the conversation. The room was so quiet that he heard the click of her impressive heels as she walked up to him, a beer in one hand and a cocktail in the other.

J.R. didn't want to look at her. He didn't want to see the face of the woman he thought he could trust and know that he'd been wrong. She'd slept with Levinson—he couldn't get his head around that, and he couldn't get past Levinson's claim that Thalia would do anything—everything— to sign him.

Did that include making him fall in love with her?

Had he ever been a bigger idiot? Had he thought that she'd

been different, that she'd actually cared about him? Or had it all been about the movie, the money?

Had it all been an act?

"You said you had him signed, sealed and delivered," Levinson said to Thalia. He could have cut glass with his voice.

This was the true soul of the man, the one who killed careers and destroyed people because it was easy and fun. This man was the living embodiment of why J.R. had left Hollywood in the first place. He never should have come back. Not even for a woman.

Not even for Thalia.

"I said that—"

Levinson cut her off. "There are no excuses. This is what I get for taking pity on a brainless whore like you. You make promises you can't keep." He snorted, his eyes glittering with the kill. "Mark my words, you couldn't screw enough people to get another job in this town. No one wants to work with a failure."

J.R. wasn't sure what happened next. Either he flipped over the table and then Thalia dropped both of the drinks, or she dropped the drinks as he flipped over the table. Didn't matter so much in the long run. The drinks were dropped and the table flipped, catching Levinson in the chin.

J.R. was so mad he couldn't think straight. He grabbed at Levinson with nothing but blood on his mind. Someone screamed. He got Levinson by the prissy tie, but before any satisfying punching could take place, hands were on him and he was being hauled backward.

"Damn, man," someone said, and J.R. realized it was Eli. "Knock it off!"

J.R. ignored him and focused on getting his arms free. He could still land a good blow, if he could just get back to that tapeworm of a man.

The next thing he knew, he was picked up and was bodily

hauled down the stairs. When he realized that each appendage had at least one guy holding on to it, he knew his chance to kill Levinson with his bare hands had passed. The club was now entirely silent, and as he was dragged out the door, he saw a whole bunch of people holding up phones.

He was in big-time trouble, and he knew it. The anger bailed on him as fast as it had rushed in, and was replaced by a sinking pit in his stomach. This was way worse than being kicked out of Denny's bar for a few months. This was probably going to screw up the rest of his life.

His vision cleared enough to see that a beautiful woman in a striking red dress was following him at a distance. She wasn't crying, nor was she screaming or even shouting. She looked like someone had gut-shot her.

"Put me down," he demanded, although he couldn't tell if he wanted to comfort Thalia or lash out at her.

"Not happening, cowboy." In the next moment, they were out the doors, and J.R. felt himself breathe in air that only reeked a little. Then he was unceremoniously dumped on the sidewalk.

A crowd had gathered by this point. More phones, plus some old-fashioned flashbulbs, were now going off. Eli was still by him, and Thalia wasn't far away.

She told you not to come, the one rational brain cell left in his head whispered to him. But J.R. was in no mood for rational. He shoved that thought aside. Hard.

Eli was talking. "I don't think I've ever seen that old fart look as scared, man!" He thwacked J.R. on the back. "Half of this town has dreamed of getting the old man on the chin, but no one else has had the balls!"

"Move." Thalia made it to them. "Walk."

"I'm not going anywhere with you. You lied to me."

"Not here," she whispered, but it was too late. People were crowding in on them, and the name James Robert Bradley rode lead on the wind.

The situation kept getting worse. J.R. knew he was spiraling out of control, but he was powerless to stop it. He hated the feeling of being unable to control himself, his life. But that was where he was at. Out of control. "You slept with *him?*"

"Not *here*," she said again. He heard the plea in her voice, but he couldn't do a damn thing about it.

"Yo, man, we gotta get you off the street." Eli had him under the arm and was hauling him somewhere. "Everyone's watching."

"His stuff is at my place," Thalia said, her voice breaking.

He heard the hurt, but he didn't want to care. Caring about her had recently become a painful thing. Too painful. He couldn't take it. He didn't want to feel anymore. "I'm not going anywhere with you. You lied to me," he said again.

"J.R., please—can we talk about this anywhere else but here?" A tear spilled over, but he had no way of knowing if it was real or just another act.

"I'll follow you to your place," Eli said, shoving J.R. toward an expensive-looking car.

"No." He stood up and shook Eli off. *"No."*

Another tear raced down her cheek. It wasn't working. He wasn't letting her make him feel guilty. He wasn't going to feel a damn thing for her, even if it killed him.

"Please, J.R. All your things."

He stood up straight and glared at her. He'd let himself get used, and for what? He'd destroyed everything he'd worked for, everything he'd built, because he thought he'd fallen for a woman.

He looked her in the eyes, trying so hard not to feel anything. "There's nothing there that I can't replace."

He didn't feel like crap when she choked and buried her face in her hands. He didn't feel like the world's biggest ass when he slid into Eli's car. He didn't feel like he was as bad as Levinson, or worse.

As Eli put the pedal to the metal for parts unknown, J.R. only knew one thing.

He didn't want to feel anything.

Fifteen

"Can I get you a snack, sweetie?"

Thalia did her best not to roll her eyes at her mother. As if another bowl of potato chips would make everything all better. "No thanks, Mom."

She'd been visiting, as Mom insisted on calling it, for a week now, and Mom was doing everything but coddling her. Mostly, it was driving her nuts. She'd lived by herself for so long that having to share a bathroom with a woman who had a shaky definition of privacy and having to sleep in a twin daybed with a ruffled duvet seemed like insult on top of injury. However, homemade meals, a shoulder to cry on and the kind of unconditional love that didn't exist in Hollywood went a long way. Thalia could use a little coddling after her collapse, so she worked on overlooking the irritating parts.

Only two weeks had passed since life as she knew it had ended on the sidewalk outside a club. She'd tried to stick it out in Hollywood, but with each day that passed, it had become that much clearer that there was no fixing the mess she'd found herself in. Even the baristas at her favorite coffee shop had looked at her funny. No one took her calls. The only person who responded to her emails was Levinson's personal assistant, Marla, and that was mostly out of fear that she was next on the chopping block.

Levinson was so enraged that he'd had a mild heart attack, which was another thing he was going to sue J.R. for. Apparently, the list of legal claims he had against J.R. was quite long. Not that Thalia knew firsthand, but Marla had taken to sending her private emails with hour-by-hour updates. The movie had fallen apart after her public character assassination. Clint and Morgan had both backed out as word of the fight spread around town, and once that news hit, Denzel wasn't far behind. She was taking more than her fair share of the blame, but, according to Levinson's assistant, other deals were in danger. The untouchable producer was suddenly vulnerable.

Not that the thought gave Thalia much comfort. At this point, not even Mom's homemade chocolate chip waffles did much to improve her outlook. She'd messed up in every possible way. She knew—and Mom kept reminding her—that she'd get past this. She had once before. But she was almost thirty, for God's sake. She felt a little too old to be starting over. At the age where most of the girls she'd gone to high school with were going to soccer games and school parties, Thalia was living with her mother again, unemployed and broke. The only assets she had were her high-end clothes, which she was auctioning off on eBay to the highest bidder. She tried to use the money to help buy groceries, but Mom wouldn't hear of it. Thalia had left almost everything else behind. Like J.R. had said, there wasn't much there that she couldn't replace.

The question she couldn't bring herself to answer was whether or not he intended to replace her.

So she was approaching middle age, single, unemployed,

living with her mom and had $429.34 in her bank account. This was going to go down in history as the most miserable Valentine's Day ever. "Getting past this" seemed as easy as climbing Mount Everest in flip-flops. She couldn't see how she was going to do it.

Not to mention that her heart was broken. Why hadn't she planned on the contingency of Levinson using the affair against her—against J.R.? She knew the answer. She'd let her feelings for J.R. blind her to the real danger Levinson posed to both of them.

She'd tried to keep J.R. from going to Hollywood. She knew she had, but she still couldn't shake the feeling that she should have done something more. She shouldn't have let him get on that plane, but she couldn't see how she would have kept him off it. When J.R. made up his mind, there was no unmaking it. And then he'd decided that he hated her, just like *that.* She knew she wouldn't be able to change his mind, but again she had that nagging feeling that she should have tried a little harder.

He hadn't listened to her when she told him not to come, and he hadn't listened to her outside the club. At some point, a girl had to cut her losses. And sometimes, there was nothing left to cut.

Thalia had lost everything. That was the sort of realization that made getting up in the morning hard to face, no matter how great the bacon smelled.

The doorbell rang. Thalia cringed, wishing she could be more invisible. Some resourceful reporters had tracked her down to her mother's house outside of Norman, Oklahoma, and were persistent—bordering on stalking—about getting details for resale.

"I'll get it," Mom said, casting a motherly eye over Thalia's yoga pants and sweatshirt outfit.

Hey, Thalia thought at her mother's back, *at least they're clean.* Why, she'd even showered today. She felt almost human.

She was headed back to the kitchen, to make sure that no one was trying to sneak in the back door while Mom was distracted at the front one, when Mom hissed, "It's *him!*"

That tripped Thalia up so fast she stumbled. "Him who?" Because it couldn't be the one *him* she wanted to see. It couldn't be J.R. He'd made up his mind about her.

"Him!" Mom was panicking, her hands flapping like a goose failing at takeoff. "That man!"

"I'm not here." Even as she said it, she hurried to the front door, peeking through the sheer curtains that covered the side window.

J. R. Bradley—complete with hat—stood on her mother's front porch, looking as stoic as she'd ever seen him. He was studying the tips of his boots, his expression unreadable. His face looked odd. He was growing his beard out again, and he hadn't quite got it matched up to the goatee. She looked around. No truck, just a car that was probably a rental.

Part of her ached at the sight of him. He was dressed well, in nice jeans and a heathered blazer that matched his hat. No bolo tie today, but he'd clearly put some thought into his outfit. She knew she'd missed him, but seeing him there crystallized the loneliness into a pain so sharp that she didn't think she could breathe.

"What do I do?" Mom whispered. How nice that Thalia wasn't the only one panicking.

"Tell him I'm not here. I'm out." She had on sweats and no makeup. That alone would make her hesitant to go face-to-face with the person who had been, until a few weeks ago, the man of her dreams.

But him showing up, with no other communication since he'd roared off with Eli Granger? What else could he say to her?

Unless he'd come to apologize. Although she couldn't say

why, that scared the heck out of her. What would he say? What would she say back? No. She wasn't ready for him. Not now, maybe not ever.

Mom cracked the door open. "May I help you?" Thalia had to hand it to her—she was doing a fine job acting not-panicked.

"Mrs. Thorne? You don't know me, but my name is J. R. Bradley, and I'm trying to find your daughter, Thalia." Even though he was fuzzy through the fabric, Thalia thought she saw his eyes cut to where she was watching him. She jumped back, terrified he had seen her. "Is she home?"

"No, I'm sorry. Thalia's not here right now." Mom even managed to sound a little sympathetic. Maybe that acting thing ran in the family.

"Do you know when she'll be back? I've got some things to say to her, and I'd like to say them in person."

Thalia's mouth ran dry as she waited to hear what her mother would come up with. Was he here to apologize? He'd said so himself—he wasn't real good at apologizing. It didn't seem likely that he'd come all this way to tell her off again. The J.R. she knew had a short temper, but he wasn't intentionally cruel. He wouldn't have come a few extra thousand miles to break her heart a second time.

She hoped, anyway.

"She's at a job interview at the local television station. I'm not sure when she'll be back."

Not shabby, thought Thalia. Probably better than anything she would have come up with.

A moment of silence followed, and Thalia realized she was holding her breath. What if he wouldn't leave? Or worse, what if he did?

J.R. cleared his throat. "Will you tell her I stopped by, please? Tell her to call me? My number hasn't changed. She should still have it."

"I'll pass the message along." Mom shut the door, then sagged against it. "Was that okay?" she whispered.

Thalia nodded, but she was paying attention to what was going on outside. J.R. stood there for a moment before he glanced back to where Thalia hoped the curtains were hiding her. Then he turned around, took two steps down the stairs—and stopped. There, on the sidewalk, stood a man with a camera. The flash was going at top speed.

Paparazzi. In Oklahoma. Snagging photos of a cowboy. Everything about this seemed wrong.

The words were muffled, but she could piece together what was happening. J.R. was telling the photographer to stop, the photographer was ignoring him and J.R. was getting mad.

"Damn it," she muttered, shoving her feet into the closest pair of shoes she had, a ratty pair of sandals that perfectly complimented her look. She knew where this would end up. J.R. would wind up breaking the man's camera, and there'd be another lawsuit. "When will he realize the whole world is not a honky-tonk?"

"Honey?" Mom hadn't moved from the door. "What are you doing?"

"Trying to keep the cops from getting involved." With a final reproachful look, Mom stepped to the side.

Thalia was out the door, trying to ignore her vanity. It wasn't hard, given that J.R. was actively attempting to grab the man's camera. Was physical violence far behind? "Hey!" At the sound of her voice, both men froze in mid-lunge-and-dodge. "What's your name?"

"George," the man said, taking a cautionary step away from J.R.

For his part, J.R. was dumbstruck. His mouth hung open as he watched her close the distance between them. She wanted to think that he was happy to see her, but she wasn't sure.

"You got a buyer for this photo?" she asked George the paparazzo.

"TMZ," he replied, looking nervous. *Must be new at this, despite the expensive camera,* she thought.

"Here's the deal, George. You get one photo of the both of us, and then you get off my mother's lawn. If I see your face around here again, well, I can't be responsible for what happens next." She pointedly looked at J.R., whose hand still hung midgrab. "Deal?"

George shifted from one foot to the next, not sure if this was something that was done or not. "Are you serious?"

"Do I look serious? Here." She stood next to J.R., lowering his hand and placing it around her waist. "One shot, George. Make it count, because he's a card-carrying member of the NRA."

George lost a little of his color, and Thalia noted with satisfaction that his camera shook as he focused the shot. "Is smiling part of the deal?" he asked, the terror in his voice obvious.

"No," J.R. said.

"Thought you used to be this great actor," she muttered under her breath while she tried to strike a pose that would hide everything about her appearance. Which was a colossal waste of time—nothing about the way she looked right now was salvageable. But this was the deal.

J.R.'s hand pressed against her side, and she swore she felt the heat through her sweatshirt. "You're home," he said through clenched teeth while George focused his camera.

"You're here," she replied.

Then George said, "Smile?" and took his one shot. "Thanks."

J.R. half lunged at George. "Get," he growled, and George got. Fast.

Which left Thalia and J.R. standing on her mother's lawn, arm in arm. For a second, neither of them moved. Moving would mean dealing with what had brought him here, and she still didn't think she could handle it. Whatever it was.

J.R.'s chest rose with an extra-deep breath. "You're good at that."

"Good at what?" She refused to look at him, even though she was touching him.

"Handling those kinds of situations."

What the hell. If this was an apology, it was a piss-poor one. Suddenly, she realized why she wasn't ready to talk to him. She was freaking *furious* with the man. "You mean the kinds of situations where people treat you like a commodity instead of a person? Yes. I'm familiar with the protocol. Unlike some people I know."

She felt, more than saw, his shoulders slump. Fine. He'd attempted to apologize, and she'd, well, she'd heard him out. They could be done now.

She disengaged herself from his arm and headed back into the house. She wasn't surprised in the least to hear his footfalls behind her, but she was too mad to care.

"Ma'am," J.R. said behind her, and she swore she heard him tip his hat to her mother.

"Hello again. Thalia, I'll…get some coffee?"

Right. A grown woman probably didn't want her mother in the room while she hashed out her last failed affair. "Thanks, Mom."

For lack of anything better to do, she sat down at one end of the dining-room table. She was so mad at J.R. that she was having trouble not yelling at him. But she was familiar with the protocol, so she waited until he took a seat. Of course he took the one closest to her. "What brings you down to Norman?"

"You."

At that moment, Mom bustled into the dining room with coffee and fresh cookies on a silver tray. "There you two go. Is there anything else I can get you?"

"Mom," Thalia said, feeling like a fifteen year old again.

"Mrs. Thorne, thank you. This is wonderful." J.R. looked

to her for approval. Well, what did she know—he could pull off some social graces when he put his mind to it. "You have a lovely home."

Hand to God, Mom blushed like a schoolgirl. Thalia was seconds away from rolling her eyes. "Oh, you're welcome, Mr. Bradley. I'll just…be in the kitchen if you need any more coffee."

Neither of them said anything until Mom was out of sight. Thalia knew she was still listening, but at least she wasn't hovering over them.

They sat in silence, neither of them apparently knowing how to start. Thalia was still reeling from the realization that she was mad at J.R. She'd spent the last two weeks being upset with herself for not doing a better job of controlling the situation, and she hated Levinson. She hadn't allowed herself to put some of the blame on J.R.

Until now, that was.

"I got a box of my things." J.R. took one of the cups of coffee off the tray, but he didn't drink it. "No return address, no note."

She'd mailed his stuff to him on her second-to-last day in California. She'd almost thrown it all in the trash, but she couldn't get rid of him that easily. "You were expecting a note?" He nodded, and that made her mad all over again. "If you think I'm going to apologize, well, think again."

"Wasn't expecting an apology." Then he got up and stood in front of the large picture window. Not looking at her, she noted. Maybe now they were getting somewhere. "I was kind of hoping for an explanation."

"What was I supposed to do, J.R.? If I told you that I'd had an affair with Levinson, you would have thought less of me—which you did when you found out. If I didn't tell you, you'd think I was lying to you when you did find out—which also happened. There was no way for me to win in this situation. Either way, I come off looking like Levinson's whore, when what happened nine-plus years ago was none of your business anyway."

When he didn't say anything, she kept going, if only so she didn't have to hear the painful silence. "I had an agent who was getting me into parties. I met Levinson. Of course I knew who he was, but you've got to remember—there were no smartphones back then, and if I wanted to get on the internet, I had to go to an internet café. I couldn't even afford dial-up. I had no way of knowing he was married. Yes, I slept with him, of my own accord." She couldn't believe her own ears. Despite the fact that she didn't owe him an explanation, here she was, explaining anyway. "I had no idea that was what he did—take advantage of eager, innocent women like me. Then his wife showed up and got me blackballed. No one would hire me. Even my agent dropped me like a rock. I was broke and clueless because I believed him when he told me he loved me and promised he could jump-start my career. If you want to hold my naivety against me, so be it. But I will *not* apologize for it."

He stood there, staring out the window so hard that Thalia began to wonder if George the paparazzo had come back, if J.R. was even listening to her. Then he said, "You don't owe me an apology. I'd like to know how you wound up working for the man who ruined your career. Can I ask that?" It could have come off as snotty or snarky, a cut meant to draw blood from someone who had seen her naked, but it didn't. It came across as an honest question.

So she gave him an honest answer. "I was about to be evicted. Days away from having to come home to Oklahoma, tail tucked between my legs. I used my last ten bucks to bribe the security guard to let me into his office, and I told him that he had to give me a job or I'd make him pay." She thought she saw J.R.'s mouth curve up in a smile, but he wasn't exactly facing her, so she couldn't be sure. "He called security on me, but by the time they got there, he'd taken pity on me, which may have been the only time he ever took pity on another living being in his entire, miserable life. Gave me a job as a gofer. I didn't sleep with him again after that, and I earned my place at the table." Had he taken pity on her, or had he seen another innocent, vulnerable young woman he could control—except instead of through sex, this time through a paycheck? Had her life ever been her own since the day Bob Levinson walked into it? "I lost my career because I made a mistake. And you know what happened to Levinson?"

"Nothing."

"*Nothing.* Just another day at the office. J.R., I never cared who you'd slept with when you were James Robert. Never wanted to know, not even a rough estimate. Why is it different for me?" She knew the answer. The infamous double standard in action.

J.R. appeared to think on that for a few seconds. "Was he always going to fire you if I didn't take the part?"

"Yes."

He held his posture—strong, stoic—for another beat, then dropped his head in something that looked like shame. "And you were willing to lose your job for me."

"Unlike Levinson, I don't enjoy destroying people." She was not going to cry, thank you very much. She was keeping her voice level, her face neutral. She was perfectly in control of herself. Too bad her tear ducts hadn't gotten the message, and blinking wasn't helping. "I didn't want to be the reason why what happened, happened."

He scrubbed a hand over his face. For the first time, she noticed how tired he looked—worn down. She wanted to ask if people had found his home, if he'd shot any trespassers. She wanted to know if he regretted the time they'd had together. She wanted to know if he regretted *her.*

"I'm…I'm no good with apologies, Thalia. Never have been."

The way his voice shook was something new, something

vulnerable. It made her want to protect him again, shield him from the dangers of her reality.

This time, she didn't. "Then why are you here?"

"I wanted to make things right."

She honestly didn't know if she should be worried or scared. He stood up straight again, his eyes focused on the world right outside her mother's house. Make things right? What sort of things? "And how are you going to do that?"

Taking a deep breath, J.R. said, "I don't know how to handle myself in public."

"I'm aware of that."

Again, she thought she saw the corner of his mouth hitch up into a smile. "And because I did such a lousy job of handling myself in public, I'm now more public than ever."

Where was he going with this? How was this making things right? How was this even close to sort of apologizing? "To the point where the Georges of the world follow you across state lines."

"Pretty much. I'm getting all sorts of offers—indie movies, TV shows, commercials even. So, I got to thinking. Minnie's not talking to me right now, and Hoss hasn't been in the mood to shoot the breeze. So I've had a lot of time to think. And I've come to the conclusion that I need a manager."

The more he talked, the more confused she got. "I thought you had an agent."

"I did. Do. I'm going to fire him, but someone really smart told me I needed to get him to sign some sort of agreement first, and I'm not sure what that'd look like."

She'd told him to sign the agent to a nondisclosure agreement. Suddenly, she felt the ground shift under her seat. She had to clutch the table to keep from falling out of her chair.

"I need someone who knows her way around Hollywood, who knows how to negotiate with those people and how to keep them happy. Someone who understands how the media works these days. Someone who knows how I get in high-pressure situations and knows how to keep me from blowing my top and doing something stupid." He turned to her then, his eyes, his beautiful amber eyes, staring at her. "I need someone more than an agent. I need someone who cares about me, who understands what I want and what I can't stand, someone who won't throw me in front of the bus."

"Under the bus," she managed to say. She had to keep holding on to the table, though. The ground kept shifting underneath her.

"Yeah, that." God, those eyes—they would be her undoing. Always. "It'd be best if that someone understood what ranching is, understood that I get up real early. It'd be best if that someone got along with my crew—my family. If that someone didn't mind a blizzard every now and then."

Wait—the conversation had taken a heck of a turn there at the end. "Are you offering me a job or—"

Before she could finish the thought, he reached into his pocket and pulled out a small, black velvet box. The kind of box that often contained jewelry. Like a ring. He stepped forward and placed it in the middle of the table. She stared at it, half expecting some man to pop up from the other side of the couch and shout, "Surprise! You're on camera!" No one did.

This was real.

"I want to make things right," he said again, taking a step back. "You are, hands down, the best thing that has ever happened to me, and I did wrong by you. You showed me that I didn't have to hide from my past, didn't have to be ashamed of the things I'd done a long time ago. You showed me it didn't change the man I am now."

Thalia wanted so badly to have a smart-aleck comeback, something that would put him in his place, but she didn't. "That's what I wanted, too." Someone who wouldn't hold her mistakes against her.

He nodded. Or at least, she thought he did. She couldn't rip her gaze away from that small black box. "I should have trusted you, listened to you, stood by you and *protected* you from Levinson. That I didn't…" His voice broke, and it took him a second to get himself back under control. "It's killing me, Thalia. That's what the old me would have done—tuck tail and run. That's not who I am anymore. I'm a man who takes responsibility for his actions. I screwed up. I let myself get sucked into that world and I didn't give you the benefit of the doubt. I failed you when you needed me. I won't let that happen ever again. I'm asking for another chance to prove to you that I'll take care of you."

She sat there, stunned. For a man who wasn't so good at apologizing, he'd made one of the better ones she'd ever heard, either in real life or on film. When had any man ever been so honest and taken his share of the blame? She couldn't recall anyone, short of her grandfather, who manned up like this. Who manned up for her.

She reached for the little box, but before she touched it, she pulled her hand back. He was right—he'd screwed up, big-time. All the heartfelt apologies in the world didn't mean he automatically got another chance to break her heart.

"What if I say no?"

J.R. stood there, his expression almost unreadable. Then he took his hat off and ran a hand through his hair. "Then I will take responsibility for that, too. But the offer stands."

She knew she was pushing her luck, but what the hell. She was in the negotiation of her life. "Which offer? The job or the marriage?"

He held his hat in front of his chest like a shield. "The job offer stands. I need a manager." That statement sent a wave of disappointment through her, but then he said, "I'm not so much offering you a marriage as I am asking you to marry me, Thalia."

She didn't know what she expected when he moved—maybe he was going to retract the ring?—but before she knew it, he was on both knees in front of her. "You make me real,

Thalia. I don't know how you do it, but when you're around me, I'm a real person, the man I always wanted to be. These past two weeks without you…I haven't felt real. I haven't been right because you're not with me and I'm not with you and it was all my fault. Even if you say no, the offer stands. There'll never be another woman like you. Not for me." He shut his eyes and swallowed, a single tear escaping to run a trail down his cheek. Thalia wiped it away before it got lost in his beard. At her touch, he opened his eyes. He held her hand to his face, where his facial hair pricked at her skin. It made her feel alive again. The sensation drove away the fog she'd been lost in for the past fourteen days.

"Will you marry me, Thalia? Will you give me another chance to be the man you deserve?"

Now how was she supposed to negotiate with that? She couldn't. It was that simple.

"What if I say yes?"

He smiled then, the real one that melted her heart in the middle of a blizzard, as he scooted closer to her, still on his knees. He looped his arms around her waist, making it the most awkward hug ever, but she didn't care. He would always be her undoing, but that wasn't a bad thing. In fact, it might be the best thing to ever happen to her. "Then we can be on a plane by tonight. We can go home, you and me."

She looked around her mother's small house. She didn't have much here, but she still needed to get her things in order. "I might need a day or two."

"Then I'll wait." He reached up and cupped her cheek in his hand, pulling her down to his lips. "There's someone here I can't replace."

* * * * *

REQUEST YOUR FREE BOOKS!

2 FREE NOVELS PLUS 2 FREE GIFTS!

ALWAYS POWERFUL, PASSIONATE AND PROVOCATIVE

YES! Please send me 2 FREE Harlequin Desire® novels and my 2 FREE gifts (gifts are worth about $10). After receiving them, if I don't wish to receive any more books, I can return the shipping statement marked "cancel." If I don't cancel, I will receive 6 brand-new novels every month and be billed just $4.30 per book in the U.S. or $4.99 per book in Canada. That's a savings of at least 14% off the cover price! It's quite a bargain! Shipping and handling is just 50¢ per book in the U.S. and 75¢ per book in Canada.* I understand that accepting the 2 free books and gifts places me under no obligation to buy anything. I can always return a shipment and cancel at any time. Even if I never buy another book, the two free books and gifts are mine to keep forever.

225/326 HDN FVP7

Name _____ (PLEASE PRINT)

Address _____ Apt. #

City _____ State/Prov. _____ Zip/Postal Code

Signature (if under 18, a parent or guardian must sign)

Mail to the **Harlequin® Reader Service:**
IN U.S.A.: P.O. Box 1867, Buffalo, NY 14240-1867
IN CANADA: P.O. Box 609, Fort Erie, Ontario L2A 5X3

Want to try two free books from another line?
Call 1-800-873-8635 or visit www.ReaderService.com.

* Terms and prices subject to change without notice. Prices do not include applicable taxes. Sales tax applicable in N.Y. Canadian residents will be charged applicable taxes. Offer not valid in Quebec. This offer is limited to one order per household. Not valid for current subscribers to Harlequin Desire books. All orders subject to credit approval. Credit or debit balances in a customer's account(s) may be offset by any other outstanding balance owed by or to the customer. Please allow 4 to 6 weeks for delivery. Offer available while quantities last.

Your Privacy—The Harlequin® Reader Service is committed to protecting your privacy. Our Privacy Policy is available online at www.ReaderService.com or upon request from the Harlequin Reader Service.

We make a portion of our mailing list available to reputable third parties that offer products we believe may interest you. If you prefer that we not exchange your name with third parties, or if you wish to clarify or modify your communication preferences, please visit us at www.ReaderService.com/consumerchoice or write to us at Harlequin Reader Service Preference Service, P.O. Box 9062, Buffalo, NY 14269. Include your complete name and address.

Can one wrong turn lead to happily ever after?

2012 So You Think You Can Write winner

Kat Cantrell

presents

THE THINGS SHE SAYS

Available March 2013 from Harlequin Desire!

The only thing worse than being lost was being lost in Texas. In August.

Kris Demetrious slumped against the back of his screaming yellow Ferrari and peeled the shirt from his damp chest.

What had possessed him to drive to Dallas instead of fly?

A stall tactic, that's what.

He sighed as bright afternoon sun beat down, a thousand times hotter than it might have been if he'd been wearing a color other than black.

Just then, a dull orange pickup truck, coated with rust, drove through the center of a dirt cloud and braked on the shoulder behind the Ferrari. After a beat, the truck's door creaked open and light hit the faded logo: Big Bobby's Garage. Cracked boots appeared and *whoomped* to the ground. Out of the settling dust, a small figure emerged.

"Car problems, Chief?" she drawled as she approached.

Her Texas accent was as thick as the dust, but her voice rolled out musically. She slipped off her sunglasses, and the world skipped a beat.

The unforgiving heat, lack of road signs and the problems waiting for him in Dallas slid away.

Clear blue eyes peered up at him out of a heart-shaped face and a riot of cinnamon-colored hair curled against porcelain cheeks. She was fresh, innocent and breathtakingly beautiful. Like a living sunflower.

She eyed him. "*¿Problema con el coche, señor?*"

Kris cleared his throat. "I'm Greek, not Hispanic."

"Wow. Yes, you are, with a sexy accent and everything. Say something else," she commanded. The blue of her eyes turned sultry. "Tell me your life is meaningless without me, and you'd give a thousand fortunes to make me yours."

"Seriously?"

She laughed, a pure sound that trilled through his abdomen. A potent addition to the come-hither she radiated like perfume.

"Only if you mean it," she said. With a grin, she jerked her chin. "I'll cut you a break. You can talk about whatever you want. We don't see many fancy foreigners in these parts, but I'd be happy to check out the car. Might be an easy fix."

"It's not broken down. I'm just lost," he clarified.

"Lost, huh?" Her gaze raked over him from top to toe. "Lucky for me I found you, then."

Will Kris make it to Dallas?
Find out in
THE THINGS SHE SAYS

Available March 2013 from Harlequin Desire!

HDEXP0213

HARLEQUIN Desire

ALWAYS POWERFUL, PASSIONATE AND PROVOCATIVE.

Rancher Marshall Grainger doesn't trust women…even though he's not averse to bedding them. Will a paper marriage with his live-in assistant make him change his ways?

Look for

BEGUILING THE BOSS

by Joan Hohl.

Rich, Rugged Ranchers:
No woman can resist them!

Available In March wherever books are sold.

**Look for upcoming titles in the
Rich, Rugged Ranchers miniseries.
Available January–June 2013**

HARLEQUIN *Desire*

ALWAYS POWERFUL, PASSIONATE AND PROVOCATIVE.

Elite wedding planner Scarlet Anders is about to enter into a marriage of her own with the entrepreneur Daniel McNeal. Too bad she doesn't remember how she got there....

Look for

A WEDDING SHE'LL NEVER FORGET

by Robyn Grady

Available March 2013
wherever books are sold.

Daughters of Power: The Capital

In a town filled with high-stakes players, it's these women who really rule.

Don't miss any of the books in this scandalous new continuity from Harlequin Desire!